RICHARD NKRUMAH-AMOS is a Ghanaian by birth. He completed Sammo Secondary School, Cape Coast, in 2003 before obtaining his Bachelor of Education (Social Sciences) degree (Hons.) from the University of Cape Coast in 2008.

He is a poet, playwright, novelist, short story writer, lyricist cum songwriter and a writer. He writes for the television and radio; and has also performed poetry on Metro Television and on other platforms such as the Ghana Association of Writers Book Festival (GAWBOFEST).

He is a member of the University of Cape Coast Creative Writers Association, Ghana Association of Writers (GAW) and Pan African Writers Association (PAWA). Aside writing for Children, Young Adults and Adults the author is also a teacher, motivational speaker, human rights activist; and women and children's rights campaigner.

He has attended editorial and several writers' workshops. He has also participated in many writers' competitions some of which include Ghana Poetry Prize (Ghana)—for Africa and Diaspora; Burt Award for African Literature (Ghana); City FM Writers Project (Ghana); Golden Baobab Short Story Competition (Ghana)—Africa; BBC International Radio Playwriting Competition (London)—worldwide; Yale Drama competition (USA)—worldwide; Kwani Manuscript Project (Kenya)—for Africa and Diaspora; The Brunel University African Poetry Prize (London)—for Africa and Diaspora.

ADJOVI

RICHARD NKRUMAH-AMOS

RABBI & RABBI

Published in Ghana by

Rabbi & Rabbi Publishers
P.O. Box UC 341
Cape Coast

Contact:	(+233) 269773904/ (+233) 553076297/ (+233) 505698498
Whatsup:	0249 945 190
Website:	www.rabbigh.com
Email:	info@rabbigh.com

ISBN: 978 – 9988 – 2 – 1641 – 2

Printed by:
Ucc press, Cape Coast
(03321-30861)

DEDICATION

To he who taught me
what counts in life by words and by deeds and by silence.
To the man whose thanks
can neither be expressed nor recited nor chanted.
To the man who has been
working behind the scenes since my infancy.
To the man, the one single person who—more than any other
humankind—has not only made this possible but also brought honour
and dignity to the whole process.
To the man I call brother, uncle, friend, role model...

I dedicate this book to you,

DR. BISMARK KWAO NKANSAH

Department of Mathematics and Statistics
University of Cape Coast
Cape Coast
Ghana

with all my best wishes.

ADJOVI

ACKNOWLEDGMENTS

Thank you, Prof. Kofi Anyidoho (International Poet), University of Ghana. At an International Conference, African Literary Forum, at the Kokrobite Beach Hotel in 2008, and later at your office, in your capacity as Kwame Nkrumah Chair in African Studies, and sometimes on phone you kept telling me one thing. That 'Though writing is a difficult exercise but once the desire is there you can make it if you put in some effort.' It is well with your soul, Prof.!

Thank you, Prof. Ama Atta Aidoo (of *Dilema of a Ghost, Anowa, Our Sister Kill Joy, changes and Edufa* fames). The last time we met it was during GAWBOFEST 2011. You said to me that 'You should not go home and sleep. Go and work hard and you will make it. You could also come back for any advice.' May you enjoy utmost peace from the Lord Almighty, Prof.!

Thank you, Prof. Dora Edu-Buandoh, Dean, College of Arts, University of Cape Coast. In the year 2007, I came to pour out my worry before you that 'I feel the urge to write but I am not a student of English.' You told me it does not matter. 'Young man, just get focused. Just work hard. Just read more and write anything that comes to your mind.' May Goodness and Mercy follow you, Prof.!

Thank you, Rev. Dr. Philip Arthur Gborsong for your persistent encouragement that motivated me to finish this book and other works. I liked the way you put it. 'My brother, don't stop writing. Just be writing and you will make it one day.' I also thank you for reviewing my final work. May you enjoy long life, Rev.!

Thank you, Mr. Samuel Otoo (Sammy Otoo). As a father, Author, an experienced Educationist and a born teacher, there was one statement you kept telling our class 'those days' and it still rings in my ears.

'There is nothing under the sun that man cannot achieve.' This keeps me going anytime frustration sets in. I also liked the passion with which you emphasized that, 'Eschew laziness. Laziness will only lead you to poverty.' May you grow from strength to strength, our father!

Thank you, Mr Tony Anase for going through the manuscript with pains and unparalleled alacrity.
Thank you, Rev. Father Dr. Isidore Bonabom for being my personal coach, tutor and advisor.
Thank you, Ernest Papa Ako (Esq.), Constantine K.M Kudzedzi (Esq.), Emmanuel Kojo Nannah (Esq.), Roland Atta Hamilton (Esq.), and Robert Addo (Esq.) for each being a role model.

Thank you, all the members of Ghana Association of Writers (GAW) especially Nana McAsante and *Wofa* Kwesi Gyan Apenteng, our indefatigable president. For making time to go through the final work I say, May the Lord be your guide!

Thank you, Elder Crentsil (Egya Crentsil), Seth Amos, Nathaniel Arkhurst Yamoah, Mr. William Arthur (Bro. Obentsir), Mr. Michael Adjei Amos, Frank Kwesi Enyarkoh (The Sii), Kojo Boafo, Stella Adjoa Ghansah, Sister Ewurama and Mr. Isaac Tunji, Felix Ato Amos (Scriptures), Solomon Itsiah (Ekowlē'), Mark Baffoe Yankah, Reindorf Egya Kofi Duncan, Ekua and Kweku Atta (Biggy Bell), Mr. Kojo Ebiasa (Zongo), Hon. Raphael Coudjoe, Mr. Daniel K. Arthur, Kobina Amenfi Bentil, Maa Effie (Mission House), Mr and Mrs Akande (Oxford Preparatory School), Pastors Prince Agyiadu (Capito) and Stephen Ekow Amos; and also Pastor Robert Kwaku Gottah of Deeper Life Church, Cape Coast.

Thank you, Mr. Issac Aloysius Amissah (the headmaster), Mr. Kingsford Arkoh, Rev Fr. Thomas Etua, Mr. Kissi Owusu Boadum, Mr. Yaw Antwi-Boasiakoh, Mr. Jones Armstrong Hanson (Asanka*)*, Miss Felicia Arthur, Miss Comfort Agyensam, Mr. Joseph Egyir, Mr.

Roland Smith, Miss Lydia Marfo, Mr. Eric Aboagye, Mr. Evans Arkaifie (Movement), Mr. Kofi Ofori, Mad. Jemima Fynn-Walker, Mad. Hassana Yahaya, Mrs. Vida Boateng Dadson, Mad. Philomina Nyarkoh, Mr. Amos Sakyi, Mad. Stella Ogua, Mr. Ransford Aneefi, Mr. Paul Amakye, Mr. Andrews Aikins, Mr. Frank Pratt, Mr. Edu Boahen, Mr. David Marfo, Mrs. Margaret Kissi Amakye, Mr. Moses Arthur Caiaphas, Mad. Aisha Mohammed, Uncle John, Ogyele and his security team; and the rest of the teaching and non-teaching staff of Nyankumasi Ahenkro Senior High School, Assin South District, Central Region. **I appreciate all your efforts.**

Thank you, Elder Coudjoe of Church of Pentecost, (Nkwantanan Assembly, Assin Foso, Central Region), Chairman Mohammed Adeleke Tiamiyu (CHRAJ Boss, Upper East Region), Alhaji Ali Mohammed Awimbila (Director, National Service Scheme, Central Region), Alhaji Ousman Tasembedo, Peter 'Neehi Kakra' Dampson, Tema and Mr. Joseph Ato Mensah (UCC Library).

Thank you, Mrs. Paulina Yankah (Headmistress, University Practise Senior High School, Cape Coast.), Mr. Daniel Quainoo, Mr. Gideon Enoch Abbequaye, Mrs. Benedicta Asante Aboagye, Hon. Solomon Ebo Appiah and Mr. Bernard Debrah Biney (All of UCC).

Thank you, all friends and colleagues and all those who helped in diverse ways but whose names time and space failed to capture.

Truly, I could not have done anything without your prayers and support. May God richly bless all of you and give you long lives.

From your humble son,
From *the unknown servant*,

- **Richard N-Amos**

ADJOVI

FOREWORD

This book is replete with about one hundred and one themes ranging from moral, religious, social, educational, spiritual, past and contemporary issues which would be best appreciated after one had read it personally.

Nevertheless, *ADJOVI* is, basically, a biographical novel which recounts the bitter experiences the protagonist, Adjovi, went through in life. Set in Konkodeka, an imaginary village in the Volta Region of Ghana, the story unravels the bitter situations that girls go through as a result of no fault of theirs. A major problem has to do with the *"tro-kosi"* system, which is an institution among the Ewe and Adangbe people of south-Eastern Ghana. The practice is linked with certain gods and shrines and, therefore, linked with the religious beliefs and practices of the people. It involves young virgins forced to marry and serve fetish priests in shrines to atone for some evil committed by their ancestors.

Even though these enslaved virgins detest their situation, they have no choice. The above, coupled with the already poor state of some families and the male chauvinistic ideologies of the culture in which the story is set, makes life highly unbearable for girls and women for that matter. It is to bring these experiences to light worldwide, for efforts to be made to stop the practice, that the book has been written.

The book has 3 parts and 33 chapters. The story is told using the omniscient point of view, which gave the author the advantage of recounting Adjovi's experiences vividly and dramatically.

Written in very simple language, the book is interesting to read. It would serve as a guide to young adolescents and motivates them to air their views frankly without fear, instead of gleefully accepting conditions that are unfavourable for them.

Rev. Dr. Philip Arthur Gborsong
Head, Dep't of Communication Studies
University of Cape Coast
Cape Coast
Ghana.

I would not have a Slave to till my ground
To carry me, to fan me while I sleep,
And tremble when I wake, for all the wealth
That sinews bought and sold have ever earn'd.
We have no Slaves at home—why then abroad?

COWPER.

ADJOVI

PART 1

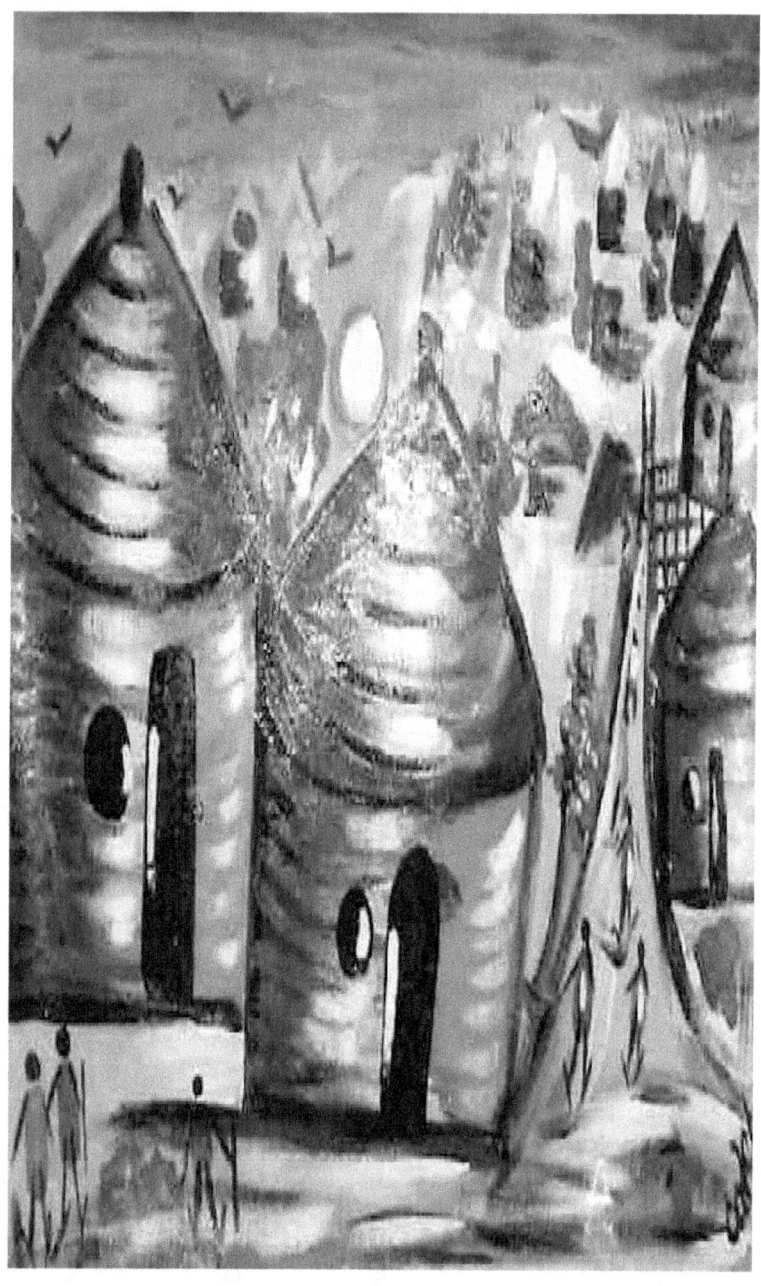

CHAPTER 1

Adjovi returned home from school to meet nobody except her father who had almost turned into a skeleton. His sickness had nearly snuffed out his life from his body. Day in day out, he cried for death to come and lay its icy hands on him. But death would not grant his wish. If he died his suffering would cease and tribulation would be no more. He said to friends who went to visit him.

Adjovi shook her head several times as she looked at how helpless her father, Efo Gogovi, had become. The old man had also not eaten for almost three days since his wife, Mamavi, attended a funeral in a distant village. Adjovi's two elder sisters, Mawusie and Sellasie, had each gone to a shrine to give some food items to their two other sisters who were serving in the shrines for the supposed offences committed by some unknown relatives of their family. Those relatives had died years before the two young women were even born.

To help his father get food to eat, Adjovi ran to the farm. She roamed the length and breadth of the farm for almost three hours. Suddenly her gaze fell on some birds pecking at some ripe mango fruits. As she brushed aside the bush with her feet to clear a path to where the mango tree stood, she heard the voices of people. The sound of the voices increased before gradually subsiding. It might be one of those Konkodeka boys looking for game. She thought as she climbed the mango tree with her sylphlike body. The place was bushy and if any of the mangoes fell it might get missing. Carefully, she plucked the succulent ones into a sack that hang on her shoulders. She put her small

3

pocket knife in one of her pockets. Next, she swung from one branch to another, still looking for more mangoes. She heard a soft cracking noise from behind. She looked around. There was nobody present. It was getting to six o'clock in the evening and insects had started buzzing around. Later, somebody sneezed. Murmur followed and what continued was a shuffling of people's feet. She panicked. She realized that she had gone far beyond her mother's farm.

As her body shook, the branch on which she stood broke suddenly with a sharp, cracking noise. She managed to clutch the tip of another branch which helped her hold her balance as her mangoes dropped from her sack to the ground. As she looked down helplessly, crying over her valued mangoes getting missing, her gaze fell on hundreds of women and young girls who were trudging towards one direction. They were carrying heavy bundles of firewood, foodstuffs, and other things. They were really tired. They wore beads around their necks and trinkets around their ankles. 'Where are these people coming from and where are they going?' Adjovi, her heart beating, whispered as she watched closely from her hideout with keen interest. The women and girls were dressed in plain white calico and every one of them had her hair shaved. Adjovi wondered why they were all dressed that way. Apart from people going for funerals she had not seen people dressed the same way before.

Suddenly, somebody laughed strangely beneath the mango tree. 'You silly daughter of Gogovi… Come, come and follow me. Follow me home. Let's go into the shrine,' the old man's speech was deep and rough like a sound of a rusty gun. Numbness caught Adjovi. She could neither talk nor move. She looked down the tree. Like the women and girls who had passed by, the man also wore bangles on his ankles with chains of very small bells hanging on his body. He had smeared his face with powder and his beard was almost down to his fat belly. 'I am Dogbe Vuga,' he laughed deviously and attempted to climb the mango tree.

But Adjovi moved up a bit. She cried and looked down at the man telling and signaling him to leave her alone. But the man again started climbing the tree, saying, 'I will go home with you this evening. This night we shall all sleep in the shrine together.' Frogs croaked in their numbers. How would she get a schola

rship to enter a senior high school should she be caught and taken to the shrine? Silently, Adjovi recited Psalm 91 in her head. With courage she jumped down from the tree and started running away.

As she sped along, the man chased her with a sword. But suddenly, the level ground on which Adjovi had walked had changed dramatically. The lowland had now turned into a ridge. As she ascended and descended the undulating chain of hills, the man still pursued her, giving her no breathing space at all. She ran and fell and got up, tripping over stones and stumps of trees several times until the man stopped chasing her for some time. She took refuge under the base of one of the hills. She was coughing, panting and gasping for breath.

But the strange man's voice came from the summit of the hill under which Adjovi was hiding. 'You are my wife... you are my wife... Adjovi, don't run away. You are my wife...' Adjovi recited Psalm 91 once again. She dived into the bush and ran for about fifty meters where a tree stood. She successfully climbed the tree but just when she raised her head to move into the branches she paused instantly. There was a big python up there ready to strike. Her cloth that tied her breast and waist were soaked with a mixture of sweat and dirt. She started getting down slowly so that the snake would not attack her. She looked down under the tree only to find a big lion lying down under the tree. The predator had stayed close to the ground with its legs bent and was ready to spring on the poor young girl. 'N-no… N-no…N-no…' Adjovi shouted and cried.

'What's wrong, Adjo? What's wrong with you? Adjo, are you all right?' Her cry made Sellasie and Mawusie wake up. They put more kerosene into the lantern. They turned up the light to see how their younger sister's body and mat had been soaked with sweat as she sat breathing helplessly on her mat. In the morning she would go and tell Eyram, Awoézo's wife. Could the woman put Adjovi's fears to rest?

CHAPTER 2

The next day was Sunday. The atmosphere in Konkodeka was cool and serene. Parents and children were on their usual duties. They were fetching water, cooking and doing other things. While a few prepared for church, others were also getting ready to look for a vehicle to go and sell their fish outside the village. Indeed, it was a village of wonderful people.

Konkodeka was a village on a branch road and getting a bus or a taxi to the nearest village was difficult. During the raining seasons the road turned muddy and impassable. No vehicle bothered to come to the village. A dusty street divided the village into two halves. At the outskirt of the village was a big tree under which people stood and sat to wait for vehicles to Keta and other places. Closer to this place was a *blue kiosk* where people went to have a drink of palm wine or akpeteshie. The market was in the middle of the village, a few meters away from the public toilet. The toilet was operated by Daavi Oboshie, a very fat, bulky woman. At one end of the village was the Quick Prosperity Miracle Church. There was also a shrine just opposite the church. In the afternoon the children were busy on the playing field of the school. They played football without boots or jerseys.

That morning, Awoézo stood in front of his dressing mirror for a couple of minutes. He examined his moustache before tucking his long sleeves shirt into his tight-fitting old-fashioned pair of trousers. Actually, he was not going to church like Eyram, his wife. He was going to drink palm wine. He considered ordained priests as nefarious schemers and their followers as cunning creatures who are intent on violent civil disobedience against the unity and well-being of married couples.

Awoézo spent time attending to his personal appearance, making small finishing touches to his moustache with his bare hands. His pair of trousers was very tight at his thighs, between his knees and hips but was baggy and flowing loosely at his lower legs, below his knees and just above his ankles. The aroma of the soup that entered the room made his mouth water as he hurried to wear his shoes.

Eyram had finished cooking. But in the meantime, she was washing a cloth or two. She had finished bathing three of her children who could only wash their shiny bellies that reflected narrow beams of light in the afternoon when the sun hit on them. The children and their mother were preparing for church. They had to be fast else they would be late. If the morning angels come to sprinkle fresh blessing and anointing on the congregation, they would miss that opportunity. It was also a special day for children. Resource persons had been invited to come and talk to the children of the church on the need to respect their parents and the elderly. Efo Agbenaza's wife would also come to sing one of her melodious, soul-touching songs. Anytime that woman sang, witches and wizards, according to people, vanished within seconds.

Awoézo stormed out of his room smiling to a delicious *akple and fetridetsi*. He clutched a table from behind a palm tree that stood fifteen meters away in front of the semi-detached hut. On the left was a hen coop. On the right was an enclosure attached to the end of the building where Awoézo kept his goats and sheep. The aroma of the okro soup tickled his nose. He whistled with pleasure and salivated right away. He sat on a stool, leaning against the wall, below the window sill. Waiting impatiently to be served, he patted at his lips with a napkin and then gave a broad smile.

Eyram served all her six children as she breastfed her newly-born baby who sat on her laps. Perhaps that was her last one. But would her husband agree?

The children bent their plates at various angles. They ate the food as quickly as they could… as if it was their last supper. Two dogs crouched closer, one from the kitchen behind and the other from under the table in front of Awoézo who had just finished washing his hands. He had already opened two buttons of his shirt and was now loosening his tight belt to allow for free movement of his belly to take more food.

Awoézo's eyes shot up in amazement. He kept smacking his lips and stroking his beard. But there was nothing coming. No food for him? 'What do you think you are doing, Eyram?' He blew out his contempt forgetting the popular saying in the village that 'Litigation about food is done in the head'. Meanwhile, Eyram failed to utter a word. She scooped a handful of the *akple*, dipped it into the okro soup and put it inside her mouth. She then looked at her baby's face, smiling and humming a lullaby for him. And so mother and children ate. Awoézo's face changed. He should be fast and take consolation in the leftovers—of his favourite meal prepared from maize and cassava dough—before the worst happen.

A few minutes later, Eyram sent Koku, her eldest child, to go and call Adjovi who stayed just a stone's throw from their hut. She asked him to go and tell the young girl to come for the small food left in the cooking pot. This was another blow to the stomach of the science teacher because he was waiting to use the leftovers if his wife and children went to church.

Adjovi, sometimes, came to help Awoézo's family to do their morning chores—washing of plates, sweeping and fetching water. She did almost everything except laying Awoézo's bed. This was an act that Sister Saviour Savi, their Sunday school teacher had warned all the girls in the church never to do for any other man—not even responsible married men they trusted most. Sister Saviour had been warning the young girls time without number to desist from such an act if they were indeed doing it. She had been warning them because of an incident that a beloved teacher narrated to her class during her student days at Aggrey Memorial Zion Senior High School at Brafoyaw near Cape Coast. The story was about how one most trusted married friend abused that teacher's only daughter. That family friend who had a wife and children sometimes asked her innocent daughter to lay his bed for him. But eventually he raped and put her in the family way. This made her drop out of school. That intelligent girl now sells kenkey at Yamoransa junction.

As soon as Adjovi came, Eyram dressed and picked her bible. With her baby strapped at her back, she headed for the church premises where Pastor Nigel Sean Ben-Acquaah had just started preaching. The rest of her children followed in a queue. Meanwhile, Awoézo stood up and blocked her way. He would not allow her to go anywhere. Eyram took advantage of her huge frame of body and pushed him aside.

'Why have you changed so suddenly in your behaviour, Eyram?' Awoézo complained, tightening his loose belt. 'Why… why… why… why, oh, why? Why do you do this to me, Eyram?' He threw his hands helplessly in the air. 'Why do you think I married you, eh? Is it not the duty of a wife to cook for her husband, eh? Be careful, Eyram be careful. I'm not ready to shed blood this morning.'

Eyram looked at her husband from head to toe. She stood akimbo, and then pulled Koku who was feeling sorry for his father. 'Why… why are you also my husband? Tell me…' She tightened the cloth she had used to staple her baby at her back. 'No… sorry. Why are you *our* husband? What do you use your "pay" for? Tell me, Awoézo.'Awoézo's nose and eye brows twitched several times. He was angry and disappointed.

'When was the last time you gave me and your children any house keeping money?' Shouting, Eyram continued. 'When was the last time you gave me and your children any money? Look at the kind of clothes that the wives of your fellow teachers wear. Look at Mrs. Kafui…'

She left for church with her children. Awoézo was speechless. Shaking her head, he went and dropped down at the corner of his hut.

CHAPTER 3

The morning assembly was characterized by several inspections. Jedidiah, the school prefect, came to check the finger nails of his colleagues. Johnny Biba—the English teacher and master on duty—went round to inspect the teeth and socks of each student. Mr. Fred Otoo-Mensah, the headmaster, came to give some special announcements.

Just after the students were dispersed for their various classrooms, Awoézo surfaced from behind them. He made threatening steps towards the Form 1 block where Biba had parked his bicycle. While a few students suspected something bad, the rest giggled. They pointed their finger at him, saying '*Hold-My-Thighs*' is coming… *Hold-My-Thighs* is coming.' They wondered because it was unusual to see him early morning on Mondays except when he was on duty.

According to the school time table Awoézo's first period on Monday started after first break—10:30 a.m—and in Form 2 class. Due to this arrangement he was a habitual late comer on Mondays. At cock crow he would wake up and go to his farm. Sometimes, he would work in his backyard garden—which was close to the school—before returning home to prepare to go and teach. In spite of this many serious students liked him because of his teaching skills. He used improvised materials and cited interesting anecdotes to make them understand his lessons. No serious student would want to miss his lessons.

Awoézo searched desperately around the school compound, looking for Biba. Biba had stormed out of the staff common room and was walking towards the form one block.

Biba had the first two periods. The two teachers met. They talked for about fifteen minutes. Here, he asked Biba to allow him to use his first two periods. Biba, a peaceful man, readily granted Awoézo's request. He walked back to the staff common room while Awoézo walked in to teach.

'Good morning class,' Awoézo greeted as he tried to force some false smile.

'Good morning, Sir,' the students responded, looking at one another's faces.

'How're you all?' Awoézo looked round the classroom. There was dead silence as he started looking at one particular direction. It was because of one particular boy that he had come to school that morning to convince Biba to swap his periods with him.

'We're all fine, and you?' The students responded with mixed feelings.

Awoézo smiled. 'I'm also doing great. In fact, I'm as fit as a fiddle and as fine as a refined gold that had gone through its processes of purification.' He coughed, his moustache twitched. 'I'm also as clean not as Captain George Maclean that Mr. Torsu might have taught you in Social Studies. I'm as clean as water whose sediments have been settled at the base by the application of alum. The children were confused about the word *alum*. When he realized this, Awoézo added, 'It is a colourless crystalline solid that is used in water purification.' The students were no longer confused but amused at how their Science teacher had bemused them. Their lesson had not yet started because that was not why Awoézo had come to the class.

'Sir,' Godson Dzinyela, the class prefect, also the most intelligent boy in the class got up and asked. 'What is the meaning of *astringents*?' Awoézo did not want to answer

13

because it was not in their syllabus. But he was too afraid to lose his popularity. Wasn't it true that the students might gossip their way home that Awoézo of all people knew nothing about astringents? For this reason he simply described an *astringent* as 'substance that drew tissues together.' But another question followed.

'Sir,' Godson asked again. 'Please if astringents draw tissues together, what then is a *tissue*?'

'*Tissue*...' Awoézo said. His gaze now fell on Fafanyo, the boy because of whom he had forced to be in that class that morning. '*Tissue* as a word has a lot of meaning. However, tissue in Science or Biology refers to organic body material in plant or animal cells that are similar in form and also perform similar function.' He seized the opportunity to explain because he would teach it the next term. 'There are four basic types of *tissues*. We have *nerve tissue, muscle tissue, epidermal tissue* and...and... and *tissue*.' The students were expecting the fourth answer. But he told them. 'Go and find out the last one. It is your assignment.' He moved away from where he stood to the left corner of the chalkboard where a clock hanged loosely on a rusty nail. He was trying hard to remember the last type of *tissue* because he himself had forgotten. He had not prepared for that.

Quickly, Godson got up again. He added, '*Connective tissue*.'

Awoézo opened his eyes in wonder. 'What do you think you are trying to say?'

'Our assignment, Sir... The other type of tissue... Sir.' The students clapped for Godson, their class prefect. 'Papa Aganu taught me some time ago, Sir.'

14

'Y-your what...? Ass-ign-ment? Do we do assignment in class?' Awoézo turned to face the chalkboard. He whispered to himself. 'There are witches and wizards in this class... devils advocates. I have to be really careful. I must prepare very well from now onwards else this Godson boy and his cohorts might disgrace me one of these days.' Spontaneously the students exploded with deafening applause, bringing the whole class to life once again. Awoézo stopped smiling. Innocent, the chalkboard prefect got up and said politely:

'P-please Ss-sir, w-we d-on't have Ss-science thi... this morning. W-we have E-e-e nglish. Mr. Biba is coming. He s-ss-said we have c-cla...cla...class te...te t-test this morning.' The students had prepared for the class test that morning and Innocent knew it himself very well. He knew for sure if he was not careful by twelve noon all that he had learnt would evaporate and vanish from his head into thin air. Again, he had to make amends since he did not do too well in the previous test.

Awoézo's eyebrow twitched and twitched. He, angrily, looked at the poor boy Innocent from the sole of his feet up to his forehead. Should he go forward and slap him or what?

'I'm v-very s-s-sorry, S-sir,' Innocent pleaded. This led to a spontaneous laughter in the class.

'Shut up!' Awoézo snapped, his moustache moving up and down. 'You're very s-sorry for w-what?' The K.G children were now out of their classrooms playing, and chasing one another. A few of them had also come to stand in the windows of the J.H.S classrooms, waiting for their elder brothers and sisters. Awoézo continued:

'If you were an *element* you would have been an *atom.*' He walked towards the boy. 'But even in this you could never

15

have been called the *nucleus* where you would have been dense and positively charged so that you could have been surrounded by a system of electrons. What I mean is that,' Awoézo continued. 'You would rather have been the *electron*—a negatively charged *particle* indeed. And you would have, virtually, got nothing to do. Rather, you would always be seen running errands. You would have always been going round the *nucleus*... Nonsense.' He raised his head and Fafanyo—the person because of whom he had done everything possible to be in that class—was not sitting at where he had seen him earlier on. That boy had carefully meandered his way down the desks to the other side of the classroom.

Even though a few of them were praying in their hearts that he did not ask of the assignment he had given them over the weekend, the entire students in the class were still amazed at how their teacher used that seemingly ridiculous situation to revise with them and made them really understand their lesson on *Elements* which many of them could hardly understand the first time it was taught.

Meanwhile, the whole class was pleading on behalf of their friend. Godson spoke on behalf of his classmates

'He's sorry, Sir. He won't do that again, Sir. We plead with you a million times, Sir.' Godson used an expression normally used by Biba, their English teacher.

Awoézo responded. 'Don't worry much. Innocent is my good friend. I'm just showing him how and when a child should talk or ask questions.' He coughed and sneezed. He was still looking for Fafanyo who was hiding under the desk on which Adjovi would have sat had she come to school that day. 'I can understand him (Innocent) because my deep knowledge in Science tells me he is suffering from malaria.' He then asked

Innocent to sit down. He had to hurry up else that Fafanyo boy would run away. The four empty desks in the class made him realize Adjovi was not at school. But he would ask of her later after dealing with Fafanyo.

'Class stand!' he commanded and everybody stood up at once. But Fafanyo was so clever that he got up and carefully hid behind the back of Hilda whose mates sometimes called her *Nyōnu-lolo* because of her body size. Awoézo was unable to see him but kept watching closely at the windows because he knew what that boy was capable of doing. He commanded again.

'Class sit! Fafanyo became nervous. He was not able to sit down quickly. Before he realized Hilda had sat down. Awoézo saw him but pretended he had not.

'Fafanyo, where are you?' Awoézo croaked, pushing fears into the heart of the young boy.

'It is here.' He responded.

'Fafanyo, where are you?'

'It is here.'

'Fafanyo, where are you?'

'I... I... I am... it is here...' He responded again, his voice now trailing off. The class remained as silent and quiet as the cemetery.

Awoézo's eyebrows twitched. He, sullenly, pursed his lips and rubbed his moustache with the tip of his handkerchief. He moved closer, looking mischievously into Fafanyo's eyes. He pulled the poor boy by the collar of his already torn uniform. He dug his long thumb nails into his back. 'Look at your face... *like the face of a pink sheet.*' The rest of the students burst into laughter.

Fafanyo's eyes were red. He was desperate to free himself again. But Awoézo held him tightly by the waist. Looking into

Fafanyo's eyes he said, 'Children like you should not be allowed to have it easy in life. As long as I remain a teacher in this school I will not sit on the fence for you to grow into *Suarez* so that you will use just one dirty finger of yours to deny the whole nation and continent of much-awaited glory. If I don't stop you now you will not change. With the spirit of *Suarez* developing in your genes you'll one day become a vampire. You'll be using your teeth to be biting at random innocent human beings created by God. And what will a boy gain after sucking the blood of a human being?'

Fafanyo's gaze roamed the class. The class burst into laughter once again. He looked at the few students who had come to stand at the window.

Awoézo splashed Fafanyo's face with his palm. As he made another attempt to slap him John Sackey went out to ring the bell for break. Alas, Fafanyo was saved by the bell. 'It is not over until it is over,' Awoézo said, gasping for breath. 'We shall meet again.' He pulled Fafanyo's nose. But as he tried hitting his forehead, the boy pushed him aside and jumped through the window.

CHAPTER 4

John sackey rang the bell for assembly. The students beat one another's shoulders, arms and backs playfully with their hands and bags as they ran to the assembly ground. Jedidiah, Biba, Mr. Fred Otoo-Mensah, lined up. They faced the children who had lined up to face them. Mr. Otoo-Mensah brought the register of each class. He flipped through them. He then sounded words of caution to those who had been absenting themselves to desist from that practice. He said in anger. 'They should either change or smell pepper.' Was Adjovi Gogovi Adinavi the main person that the thick and tall headmaster was talking about?

Until recently Adjovi herself liked school. Her love for school started growing barely five years ago when she repeated Class 3. She remained in class 3 that year because she failed to write the exams. She also failed to attend classes regularly. Why? Her mother had been going to the seaside with her and her two elder sisters, Mawusie and Sellasie. They bought fish, smoked and sold them at the bigger market at Keta.

Efo Gogovi had been sick for some years now, perhaps, from his uncontrolled appetite for *akpeteshie* and tobacco smoking. Sometimes some part of their profit was used to buy foodstuffs to be sent to Mamavi's two other daughters who were then serving in two different shrines in two different villages. The remaining amount was further divided into three. One was kept under Mamavi's pillow, a special private bank. Another part was used to buy food to feed the family. The last portion was given to Sellasie and Mawusie to share.

One day, when Adjovi and a few other pupils were still weeping over why they had been repeated in Class 3, they met Aganu. The old man took time to console them. He talked to them about the need to forget about the past and look forward to the future—the future where they would spend the rest of their lives.

A week later Adjovi and her friends went to play together with Godson and his sister, Lois, in their house. There was an interesting T.V program. They threw away their empty milk and tomato tins which they had picked from Mr. Dzinyela's dustbin and rushed to the living room. The midday news bulletiing was read by a well-dressed lady presenter by name Baaba Sam. It was a wonderful experience for the youngsters. Adjovi in particular was fascinated by the lady newscaster. The lady became a role model for her. Adjovi was enthused about the newscaster and everything that she did on the screen. She would be happy to be like her one day. Later, *'I Told You So'*, the first ever Ghanaian movie was screened. They watched with keen interest the various roles played by the characters like Araba Stamp, Bob Cole, Osuaborobo and others.

'Papa Aganu,' Adjovi asked him when he entered the living room. 'Did that woman who read the news a Ghanaian?' 'Yes, she is a Ghanaian,' was the reply.

Adjovi put her hands behind herself—what Sister Saviour Savi, their Sunday school teacher had asked them to do when talking with elderly people.

The old man felt happy for Adjovi's interest. 'What a person wants to be in future he or she must work very hard to achieve that objective.' He sat in a sofa and put his walking stick across his laps. He intoned. 'That woman is from Africa here, Ghana of course. She had all her education here in Ghana.'

The children nodded.

Aganu nodded one more time.

'If she is from Ghana here,' Adjovi asked again. 'Why is it that she appears on *Nyabrōō T.V? (Nyabrōō T.V* was a local television station.) Some people say in our school that it is only a *Yevu*—a Whiteman—who can appear on T.V. Somebody also said that if that person comes from Africa then such a one should be a man.' There was some noise above their head. They looked up. It was Virgin Bingo, Mr. Dzinyela's cat which was running after a mouse which had gone to hide under the ceiling of the roof.

'Well, it's a lie,' the old man shook his head. 'It's an impalpable lie. If somebody comes to tell you that it's only the Whiteman who can read the news that is not true. If you go to America right now their president is a Blackman.' Joyfully, the children clapped their hands. 'When he decided to be the president,' Aganu continued, 'many people did not believe him. But he worked very hard and now he is the president. He has showed that with education and determination one will succeed in what one has determined to do. It does not matter whether that person is black or white, man or woman. Where determination exists failure can never dismantle the flag of success.'

'Papa Aganu,' Lois asked, rummaging through the old man's sack. 'And so how come Aunte Baaba Sam is on *Nyabrōō T.V?*'

'Through learning, hard work and perseverance...'

'Through learning, e...eh?' She kept asking herself. 'So can learning make a woman appear on T.V?'

21

'Yes. If only you will take your studies seriously you can become whatever you want to be in future. You must attend classes regularly. You must read your notes everyday. You must do every assignment and exercises, class tests and examinations that your teachers would ask you to do. They are not there to disturb you. They are there to prepare you for the future.' Adjovi, Lois and Hilda were happy especially when the old man said that, 'What a boy can do a girl can equally do when given the opportunity and the enabling environment. But aside everything else never forget to make the library your best friend.' After this encounter, Adjovi and a few of his friends developed special love for school.

CHAPTER 5

The students dispersed for their various homes with joy. But the conversation about the topic *Hold-My-Thighs versus Fafanyo* hardly died from their lips. Throughout the rest of the day they wondered why a teacher and a student could engage themselves in a scuffle. Meanwhile, Fafanyo did not wait for the school to close before going home. He was not ready to answer anybody's question. He changed himself and waited for some few friends—four boys and two girls—so that together, they moved to the beach. As they waited for boats or canoes to arrive from the sea, they moved to the lagoon which was just close by. Here, they harvested their fishing traps which had caught some mudfish, tilapia, crabs and shrimps.

On weekends and holidays children of Konkodeka went to either the lagoon or the beach. They helped the fishermen whose canoes or boats had left the shore a night before and had now reached shore to unload their catch. They were given some fish by the fishermen. The fish were sold to the fishmongers. They also received fish from their own friends who did not attend school but chose to fish in the lagoon.

Sometimes, Mr. Otoo-Mensah and a few other teachers tried to catch them from the shores and bring them back to school to be punished. However, they were unable to get their hands on them. This was because Fafanyo would alert them before the teachers got to the shores. The children would then dive into the water and quickly swim away. Those who were unable to dive disembarked quickly from the canoes and boats.

They dodged behind these vessels and the teachers never got them.

Biba brought some books to class the next day. It was essay writing exercise books. Adjovi who was not in school that day had fifteen out of twenty marks. She was ninth in the class of twenty six students. After sharing the books Biba remarked, 'Adjovi has the potential. She is a potential student. She has the potential with the future smiling broadly at her. She can make it if she sits down to learn… if she sits down to read her notes.'

Right after school, Hilda went to Adjovi's hut. Adjovi was not at home. Hilda hurried to the well to fetch water so that she could come back earlier to complete her Science and Maths assignments which she was unable to finish at school. She must also prepare for the R.M.E class test the next morning.

When she was returning from the well, Hilda looked on her left. There were heaps of stones. People were standing while others were sitting and breaking big rocks into smaller pieces. Somebody called her name. It was Adjovi. She was sitting behind a heap of stones which she had started cracking before sunrise. Her white-turned-brown dress had been soaked with sweat from every part of her body. Her father's condition had reached the level that needed critical attention. Her mother would use the money earned from the sale of the stones to purchase drugs for Efo Gogovi. She would use the remainder—which was not always the case—for herself.

'It's me, Hilda,' Adjovi got up.

'Ei, Adjo,' Hilda brought down her pot of water off her head. She walked towards her friend who had taken a few steps to meet her.

'You were passing to the well,' Adjovi said. 'I called you several times but you didn't respond.' She was drenched in her own sweat as she dropped the hammer in her hand.

'I'm sorry, Adjo,' Hilda said. 'I've even been to your mother's place. I came to see why you've not been coming to school these days.'

'Well...e-eh,' Adjovi shrugged carelessly. 'I'm there. I'll be in school tomorrow... no,' she protested herself. 'No, I'll come on Thursday. Anyway, I try my best to read my notes every evening before I go to bed.'

'Thursday? No. you can't say that, Adjo,' Hilda beat her shoulder playfully. 'You shouldn't say that. We have R.M.E test tomorrow. And *Mr. Light Off* is serious about that. He said "those who would not do well would be punished." *Hold-My-Thighs* was also saying the same thing. And you also know that Mr. Fiagbe cannot be predicted. He can do class test depending on which side of his bed he would wake up from.'

'Uh,' Adjovi's face changed. 'Then I'll try and come to school tomorrow.' She wiped away beads of sweat that had formed on her forehead with her thumb. There was a rushing disturbance in the nearby bush. An object was slithering its way under the green grass. It was a python busily looking for a prey to attack. The few children who were still breaking more rocks screamed to alert everybody about the presence of the python.

'Anyway,' Hilda patted Adjovi's shoulder. 'Your English exercise book is with me. I hope you'll come for it. Won't you? Or I should bring it to you at home?'

'Well,' Adjovi heaved a long sigh of relief. Why should a young girl of her age be going through all these problems? Why should she be doing such back-breaking work to the neglect and detriment of her education? Meanwhile, Hilda's mother was by this time waiting for her water to cook.

'So have they been asking of me in class?' Adjovi asked.

'Yes,' Hilda answered forthright. 'Lois and Jedi asked of you.'

'Really? Where did you see them?'

'I met Lois and Jedi today, too. The two were chatting.' Hilda clapped her hands.

'You mean Jedidiah and Lois?' Adjovi inquired. Was there an interest? 'That may be why I heard somebody call them *"The Royal Couple".*'

'And… and what do they say…? What have they been saying about me? What are the entire students saying?' Adjovi moaned as she bowed to pick her hammer; and her head pan; and her small water bottle. Joycelyn and Olivia who were both carrying pots of water joined them. Chatting along with her friends, Adjovi trudged home. Innocent was also now coming to fetch water. He stopped along the way and went closer to the young girls.

'A-a…Aj-j…jo. S-so y-you…you ha…ha…ha…' Trying to bring out the words, Innocent whistled with his eyes almost closed. 'S-so you h-ha…ha…have sto…s-topped school? I h-have n-n-not been s-s-see-ing you.' He breathed out loudly. 'Ss-so wh-why?Adjo, why?' He wiped with his finger tears that had dropped from the corner of his left eye.

Adjovi and her friends turned their heads aside. They pursed their lips so as to avoid laughter. 'Oh! I haven't stopped coming to school. I'm looking for some money. And after my father's medicines are bought I'll buy my books… Science and Maths text books …' she yawned. Meanwhile, Hilda had spent more than two hours. Her mother was waiting for the water as well. She must hurry up and go. But she was absorbed in her friendly conversation, too. She said to Adjovi:

'But your father has a big cocoa farm elsewhere? Why don't you and your sisters go and pluck some so that you can go and sell them for money?'

Adjovi looked into the sky. She kept quiet for sometime before responding. 'My father's family members, according to my mother, have taken over the entire farm from us ever since his condition worsened.'

'But there is still some left for your mother?'

'Yes... but...'

'But what,' Hilda cut in.

Yawning, Adjovi answered. 'You know my mother attends funerals every Saturday. And she says she must have people to know that she is also a woman. And so the little money from the small cocoa farm left behind is used to sew different funeral clothes.' She turned to see whether somebody was listening to their gossip. 'When there is a funeral in our home she and all my uncles and aunts sew a particular new cloth. They don't want the situation where their dead bodies would be disgraced.'

'How did u know?' A.D Olivia and Joycelyn Edinam Tetteh asked together.

'Uncle Aglago once said so and I overheard him.' The weather was getting colder and colder. Goats and sheep trotted into their pens. Insects began to buzz around, paving way for another sunset.

'Adjo, what you are saying is true,' Olivia stopped walking, bringing down her pot of water. She sheepishly looked into Adjovi's eyes. 'My mother keeps saying that the dead must not be disgraced. For this reason she says I should go out myself, look for money to buy for myself new pair of shoes, a school bag and books. She would rather need money to buy a red cloth for the wake keeping on Friday, a black cloth for the burial ceremony on Saturday and a white one for the thanksgiving service on Sunday. Hmmn… All these'—she whispered because there was somebody passing by—'All these expensive clothes come with their bags, shoes and earrings to match.'

The conversation turned interesting when the issue of wake keeping came in. Adjovi narrated how two 'sugar daddies' who had come from the city put her two elder sisters in the family way during one big funeral in the village. She also lamented about how her sisters' pregnancies and their eventual deliveries had drained the little resources of her family.

Innocent, the only boy among the four girls, had forgotten it was now that he was coming to fetch water for his mother. He followed the girls for a while, almost back to their huts. But he stopped suddenly and ran away from them. He left the girls when their conversation led to the issue concerning their English exercise that Mr. Biba had brought to class that morning. Innocent knew his class mates would talk about the usual 'who was first…? Who had what? …' If no one brought the issue, he believed Olivia—who sat in front of him in class— would intentionally raise the issue again. She would by hook or crook wag her tongue at him and tease him for scoring low marks once again. Joycelyn and Hilda screamed. They had neither done their assignments nor studied for the class test for the next day.

CHAPTER 6

Adjovi knelt down under one of the window sills of the staff common room. Awoézo, few other teachers moved out of the room, still quarrelling over *single spine* and politicians. They were now convinced that politicians who come to promise them better salaries during campaigns back out from their promises when they win elections. It was the end of the month and the teachers in the school—especially Awoézo—were expecting mouth-watering salaries as they had been promised.

For more than six months Awoézo could hardly teach. He simply lacked the motivation to exhibit what he knew best. Anytime he tried explaining something he found himself loosely explaining how the supposed *single spine salary structure* would be like.

He just had a dream the previous Thursday. He dreamt that he had gone to the bank to collect one big bag of money. Togbui Amekudzi, the chief of the village, had then come to bow before him and was begging to polish his *Santiago shoes* for him. Fat women in and around Konkodeka were also busy clamouring for his warm embrace. But he was unable to translate his dream into reality. He woke up the next Friday morning, had a bath and powdered his armpit with talcum powder. Next, he set off to his bank at Keta to collect his salary only to return home with half his actual salary.

He became sick at once and decided not to work again. That day Awoézo and his lovely son, Koku, wept like children. Why? The man had gone to borrow money from friends and

29

money lenders. He had also bought many items on credit from the palm-wine sellers and the market women who would soon come for their money.

Before the implementation of the S.S.S.S—Single Spine Salary Structure—many workers especially teachers believed that they would smile throughout the rest of their lives. They would forget about the unnecessary comparison that their nagging wives made with the wives of some other civil servants. Some of these wives had started comparing themselves to wives of bankers and custom officers.

The amount of *Single Spine money* that was added to their previous salaries was just insignificant. Even though one or two of them had their salaries increased, majority of them had their previous salaries slashed. They complained. 'If you don't get anything good for your mother-in-law you don't cheat her.'

When the complaints were becoming too much Johnny Biba and Prosper Torsu also countered the arguments of their colleagues with what the previous government also promised yet was unable to deliver. They challenged Awoézo and the rest of their colleagues. They argued that the previous government promised zero tolerance for corruption during their political campaign but later, after winning power, came to say that corruption started from the Garden of Eden. They had promised bigger salaries for workers but later came to plead with people to tighten their belts.

According to Mr. Otoo-Mensah, 'there are two groups of students: those who look for a way and those who look for excuses. Those who look for a way must sometimes be pardoned for their little offences. But those who look for excuses must not be pardoned at all. They must rather be shown the exit of the school. They must be expelled from school since they fail to hope that they will one day make it.' For that matter Adjovi, three others, ought to be punished in order to deter their other colleagues from absenting themselves from school.

Adjovi was later asked to sweep and clean the school's lavatory for the number of days she had absented herself from school. She was also asked to weed for five days, using school hours—a punishment that the Agricultural Science teacher always objected to. This, according to the teacher, would make the young students believe that farming was a punishment which was never the case. He also argued that, 'This is one of the reasons why the youth of today are refusing to go into farming. They have already been confused right from school that farming is a punishment forgetting that agriculture is the backbone of developing countries of which Ghana is one.'

But the Agricultural Science teacher was not in the school at that moment. He was in the hospital receiving treatment for the injuries which he had sustained in a motor accident. The accident took place at Winneba Junction on the Accra-Cape Coast highway. This happened right after a similar one had occurred at Senya Breku, a nearby town, where a water tanker ran into people making merry at the road side. In that accident about thirty people were killed and many more were injured. A month earlier all the passengers on board a 207 Benz bus had died on the spot on the Cape Coast-Takoradi highway. The unfortunate event took place when two of the tyres burst. The bus ran into a stationary articulated truck loaded with cement.

Adjovi got up from under the window sill. She knocked and entered the headmaster's office. There she cried. She knelt down again and started begging. But Mr. Otoo-Mensah would not listen to her. She, therefore, screamed. As she cried tears ran down her cheeks into the corners of her mouth. Her sorrowful tears touched the heart of the no-nonsense headmaster.

Mr. Otoo-Mensah met the teachers in his office. He discussed one or two things with them. After the brief meeting, Adjovi's punishment was reduced. She would now clean the toilet for three days and weed for two days. Right after closing she would have to go home, bring machete and start weeding. John Sackey went to ring the bell for break.

When the break was over, Mr. Otoo-Mensah asked the teachers to bring their lesson notes for him to go through them before the circuit supervisor comes unannounced to inspect them. Later, he asked them one after the other to bring the exercise books of their students.

He carefully examined the lesson notes and the students' class exercise books. With some of the exercise books he smiled and nodded in agreement but with others he frowned. When he had finished going through the books he would leave for the District Education Office at Keta to have a discussion with the District Director of Education.

CHAPTER 7

Mr. Otoo-Mensah moved back and forth from the edge of his seat. He adjusted his trousers and lowered his arms—which were clasped on his chest—onto his table. He then asked Johnny Biba to call for Innocent. The performance of Innocent Agbemo Agbenaza was far below average.

'What's wrong with you, Innocent? Why don't you want to sit down and learn, but rather choose to follow your friends to the lagoon?'

'N-no, S-ssir…Nn- no-nothing S-ssir… I…I …I d-don't go to the l-l-la-lagoon. I don't all… all… I don't a-also go to the sea, S-ssir.' He found no reason for not saying so.

'If nothing,' Mr. Otoo-Mensah said as he turned three more pages of the green exercise books in front of him. 'Then why should you score such marks. You need to buck up. You need to turn over a new leaf else…'

Innocent knelt down. He pleaded with Mr. Otoo-Mensah.

Mr. Otoo-Mensah opened his mouth. A fly flew across, almost entering it. 'Keep quiet you lazy rat!' Innocent wanted to open his mouth. But he stopped suddenly when Mr. Otoo-Mensah hit the top of his table with a cane. 'Now let me tell… and tell you again. If you don't study hard you will not be promoted to Form 2. You'll repeat the class.' He felt the knot of his bow tie he wore over his short sleeved shirt. 'No,' Mr. Otoo-Mensah changed his mind. 'You'll go back to class six.'

'B-ba- bb-ack to where? B-back t-tto cla… cla…class six?' Innocent's eyes almost popped out of their sockets. He was shocked. He was determined not to cry even though he knew the headmaster was principled and he would never go back on his words. However, he could still feel some little drops of tears tickling down on his cheeks. He would not want to repeat again for the third time running.

'And so that is for your information,' Mr. Otoo-Mensah was emphatic. But he later noticed something on Innocent's face and so he softened his stand. 'But you must try hard. The boy who says I will try will always climb to the hill top. Try and get fifty percent.'

'M-m-mas-ster,' Innocent rubbed the tears in his eyes with the back of his hand. 'And s-s-so if-f-f if s-some...s-somebody g-g-gets f-f-four...f-forty per...per...p-percent will he be repeated?' He breathed out heavily.

'Yes.'

'Wh-wh-what about f-four...f-for-forty two per per...p-percent?'

'No,' Mr. Otoo-Mensah was emphatic. He hit the top of his table with his fist. 'He will still be repeated unless he gets fifty.'

'Then I... I w-will t-tr-try and get f-for...f-forty four per...per...p-percent.'

'No.'

'Then I... I w-will t-try to get f-forty nine.'

There were whispers outside. Some students knocked on the door. John Sackey had rang the bell. It was second break. They were coming for their ball which the headmaster had seized the previous week and had promised to give it back to them that day. Before Mr. Otoo-Mensah gave them the ball he asked one of them to call Fafanyo for him. The boys said, 'Fafanyo was in

34

school this morning. But we didn't see him in class again when *Hold-My-Thighs...*' They quickly changed the name. 'We're sorry, Sir. We hadn't seen him again when Mr. Awoézo entered the class.'

Mr. Otoo-Mensah kept quiet, bobbing his head up and down. He picked a red pen from his left pocket. In his head he had now got to know that it was indeed true that the students had been calling them different names. It was also true that Fafanyo and some of his friends—one in Form 2, two in Form 1—had been calling Kafui and other teachers some names. Those other guys who were given twelve strokes of the cane each in both first and second terms for stealing or sending *apo* into the examination room were also among. Those stubborn boys had made the rest of the students call Kafui, *Mr. Light Off.* Did Mr. Otoo know this?

Mr. Otoo-Mensah was also getting to believe that he had once heard the children calling him '*Koo Sika*' suggesting that he liked talking about money. Could he have a good reason to confront them? He smiled and resumed his seat, having remembered his early days in school; having remembered how their class would give names to their teachers when their tongues had slipped or when they failed to pronounce words correctly. They would also give special names to their own mates should something happen in the classroom. 'Oh childhood days; gone were the days when we were children. Childhood days are great times to remember,' he kept smiling and saying to himself. He looked at his wristwatch and threw the ball back to the students and asked them to go. He turned back to Innocent again.

'Now tell me, young boy. What happened to your cheeks?'

Innocent rubbed his eyes before talking. A duster fell off from his hand. 'It was my mother.'

Mr. Otoo-Mensah was taken aback but was still interested. 'Your mother? Your mother who carried you for nine months in her womb? What did she do to you?'

'S-sh-she...she s-sla...slapped me?' He cried. 'He's been s-slapping me?'

'S-sla...slapped you?' She's been s-slapping you?' Mr. Otoo-Mensah's eye brows shot up in surprise.

'Y-yes.'

'How could mere slaps create blisters on your cheeks?' Realising that the boy was being economical with the truth, Mr. Otoo-Mensah used his basic psychology to get more from him. 'Tell me. I won't tell anybody.' He wrapped his arms around Innocent's shoulders. 'What happened to you?'

'E-er...er... It was my mother. She threw a box iron at me... and it touched my cheeks.' He felt his cheeks with the back of his hand. 'And the fire ran down on my cheeks and my back.'

There were hoots of motor cycle outside. The students moved one by one towards a man wearing a green overall garment which was emblazoned at the back 'GHANA POST'. The man asked of the headmaster's office before pulling out some envelopes from the metal box which was welded to the back of the big motor cycle.

'So you mean your mother did this to you?' Anger welled up in Mr. Otoo-Mensah's chest.

'Y-yes. She has been s-s-sla-pping me and knocking my h-h-he... m-my head against the window ev-vvery morning... And s-sometimes even before I w-w-wake up.' He cried.

Full of pity for the young boy, Mr. Otoo-Mensah looked up, shaking his head.

Mr Otoo-Mensah opened the three envelopes at the closing assembly, but smiled and kept their contents to himself. He would read the information in the letters to them next two weeks Wednesday after worship. He told the expectant students. As they dispersed home, the students contemplated on the content of the letters. What at all was in the letter that Koo Sika did not want them to know then? Some said they were going to be given books and computers as Mr. Otoo-Mensah claimed he had been fighting for. Others said they were going to start their athletics competition very soon. Olivia, Joycelyn, and Hilda also believed Light Off, the R.M.E teacher who doubled as the school counselor, was going to be transferred. What he had been doing or trying to do with some ignorant, uninformed souls had reached the District Education Office. The argument would continue till the letters were opened.

CHAPTER 8

Adjovi withdrew herself on the verandah. Torsu had given an assignment to be collected the next morning. She also had to weed her portion of land which was her punishment. (Any way, the punishment would stop her from going back to crack stones except on weekends.) To avoid wasting time, she went back to her own classroom and sat there alone. There, she groped helplessly under her desk. She looked for her pen which she was unable to find from neither her torn school bag nor from her straight, no-style uniform which was also torn in the armpit.

Adjovi's hand touched something. It was an envelope. Her name was on the envelope. There was a red hand sketch of a heart with a piece of arrow piercing through from one side to the other. Somebody whispered from behind her.

Adjovi turned her head. There was nobody around. As she complained to herself for misplacing her pen, the envelope in her hand fell through her fingers. She opened it. It was a love letter. Her face changed, still wondering about the person who might have secretly brought that letter. The person's handwriting was awkward as well. She tried hard to suspect the person.

House No. K/419
No. 9 Jato Street
Konkodeka
14th February, 2000.

Dear Adjo,

The brightness of the son and the whiteness of the moon has given me the opportunity to write you this letta. How're you? I hope you're fine by the Grace of God. I don't know how to even start my letta because am love you verly verly march. I am even weeping right now. If you torch my body you can feel and see am shivering everywhere. You're the only fish in my soup and I can explain to you. If Hold-My-Thighs come to class and he is teaching I don't listing. If Light Off come to class and explain how God create a woman I am always look at your face. If my father send me to go and buy akpeteshie for him to drink so that he can eat well or if he send me to go and buy cigarette I walk behind you but you don't see. Ha...ha...haaa. I laugh in my own head.

Furthermore, I saw you and Hilda three days ago and both the two of you were verly far away. I run I ran. I chase you ...aaa but I didn't see you again. Adjo, that time my mother, Daavi So-fire has gone to funerals and so my father send me to go and call his friend Daavi Oboshie, the fat woman who sell the public toilet. Adjo am love you. Am want to marry you one day. All that I have said means that am love you. Adjo, you're two beautiful. Adjo you're two much. You're my harmattan pawpaw. You're the apple in my mouth. Only God nose how march I am love you. Don't break my hat. My hat is all for you. I am buy you chewing gum and both the two of you and me will chew our chewing gum together. If you become my girl am give you money every day. Every Saturday am also give you fish. Am give you big, proper fish.

Thank you verly much for becoming my girl. Bye bye. But before I go I am kiss your hand. Mmm...m.

Yours lover boy,
Fafa.

Adjovi smiled and read the letter for the second time. She thought of tearing the letter apart but rushed through it again for the third time. Was she touched? As she picked her bag to leave the room she found her lost pen at the edge of her seat. She then sat down again, picked her note book from her bag, and looked at the first question on the chalkboard. A voice whispered again. Adjovi turned again and before she realized Fafanyo had pricked her. He touched her soft buttocks with his fingers.

'Why do you do that, eh? I hate that,' she was angry. 'This is the second time of doing this to me. The next time you do that, I'll tell Mr. Otoo-Mensah.'

Fafanyo smiled coyly, 'Am only praying with you.'

'Is that the way you play? Anyway, what do you want here? You came to school in the morning, but ran away a few minutes later. You're always the first person to go back home. Why are you still around today? Won't you go to the sea shore?' She moved back, throwing furtive glances around. Adjovi did not want anybody to see her near Fafanyo.

'Well,' Fafanyo gave a little shrug before sitting closer. 'Today am didn't go to the sea or the lagoon all because of you. *Me lō wo.* I am love you verly verly much. Yes. It's true. I am *calling a shovel a shovel.* If I didn't love you I won't used one full week to sit down and write to you my sweetletter.'

'*Dzo me!*' Adjovi hit Fafanyo in the chest and pulled herself backwards, away from him. 'Don't you ever say that again. Has your Sunday school Madam not told you about that…?'

'That what is it?' Fafanyo snapped. He was getting impatient. 'Let me also tell you. I goes to church. I am chorister. I and Efo we both are Christians.' He pushed closer to Adjovi and touched her softly.

'Please don't do that. I hate that. When did you go to church? When did you become a Christian? Have you forgotten about what Mr. Awoézo said the other day?'

Fafanyo kept quiet for some time before talking. 'Who...? You mean *Hold-My-Thighs*? What did he say?' Farmers were returning from their farms. They passed by the classroom. Their shadows entered and left the classroom. Some children too were on the field playing. 'What did he say?' Fafanyo remembered. It was about teenage pregnancy.

'Were you not in class when he was teaching *Reproduction?* When he said we could get pregnant and would not be able to complete our education when we engaged in boy-girl relationship?'

'And so what?'

'Why are you saying this, eh? Don't you know that I'm a virgin, too?'

'Everydays you're virgin. You don't know that my grandmother is also a virgin? She is a more virgin than you.' You can ask my mother and father all. We all... we are virgins.' Fafanyo was getting angry.

'So you want me to stop schooling? I'll tell Mr Fiagbe and Mr. Otoo-Mensah tomorrow.' She shouted but Fafanyo quickly pulled out two cedis from his pocket. He threw it upon Adjovi's laps. She was confused. Should she give in? She needed money badly to buy books and other things, too.

'Now I could see you don't read your Bible. You don't know any quotation.'

'Who? Me and you who know Bible? Go and read *Abraham 10:10.'*

'You mean Abraham?' Adjovi was a bit confused.'Which Abraham?'

'Abraham chapter ten verses ten.'

'And what does it say?'

'Go, read and see yourself.'

Adjovi kept quiet.

'Okay, since you now accept you don't know Bible let me teach you.'

'Okay, you say it.' She was counting the sixty six books of the Bible in her head.

'*Abraham 10:10* it say that my children, o ye my children. Be verly verly careful because "what can come can come".' He scratched through his hairs to recollect the continuation of the so-called quotation which he might have heard from one of the preachers at the market or lorry station or those who preached to passengers on *trotro* cars. 'And so my children what you did not do for your neighbor you did not do for me.' Footsteps drew closer from the corridor. It was Kafui.

Adjovi put her finger into her mouth, praying that her teachers would not pass by the room where she and Fafanyo were still sitting and chatting together. She didn't want to be associated with a recalcitrantly truant student.

'What are you still doing? Weren't you given punishment to do?'

Frozen with fear, Adjovi kept quiet. Kafui had seen her with Fafanyo that was why he was shouting. She thought.

Kafui looked round several times before moving towards Adjovi. 'Anyway, whom were you talking to? I believe it wasn't that nasty cockroach, eh?'

'N-no,' Adjovi lied, breathing out her fears. She was relieved but was still surprised as to how Fafanyo had vanished from the room. He was smart and fast as if he was at the lagoon; or at sea shore standing on people's canoes with friends who stealthily stole fish from the big brass bowls which were on the heads of the fishmongers.

Kafui stroked Adjovi's cheeks and dimples. 'Next time be a good girl,' he forced some faint, infectious smiles. 'What are you doing? You're solving Science problems?'

'Y-yes S-sir,' she bowed her head.

'I quite remember during my school days. I was always the first and best student in Science. My friends used to call me *Abraham Lincoln* because I was very good at performing scientific experiments.' He sat down beside the poor young girl.

Adjovi nodded, gently dragging herself backwards. Sister Saviour, their Sunday school teacher as well as Pastor Nigel had warned them not to sit in the dark and quiet places alone— especially with the opposite sex. *'It is dangerous. You can get pregnant. You can also go to hell.'* They would say and all the children in the church would laugh afterwards.

Gently, Kafui dragged himself closer to Adjovi, as he carefully looked around. 'Why have you not been coming to school of late, eh?'

'Er...erm...,' Adjovi was uncomfortable. 'But sir, I don't have books and... and my father is also... is also sick.'

Kafui put his hands around Adjovi's neck and started fondling her. He looked into Adjovi's eyes. She was just beautiful—slim and fair in complexion with plenty hairs on her head. When she smiled her gleaming white teeth—which were nicely arranged and evenly set apart with a small gap in her upper set of teeth—sparkled. 'My little girl, I've told you to be a good girl and you'll get whatever you need.' He breathed out heavily and started touching Adjovi in the waist. 'You have no problem. Tomorrow come for money.'

'Thank you, Sir,' Adjovi said as she tried pulling her hand from Kafui' arms. *Megawō hasi o* (Thou shall not commit adultery). Having rememberd this she started packing her books home. But the school counsellor would not allow her to go. All of a sudden, two class two boys and one class one girl entered the room. They were playing 'hide and seek' with their friends and for that matter they were looking for a place to hide. Quickly, Light Off pulled some coins from his pocket. He gave them to the children. The children happily left the room.

Fafanyo whispered to himself. 'What does Light Off want to do with *my chick*, eh? He will go to hell.' The three children who had been given coins went and showed the money to their friends who also came to ask for some. Kafui gave them also some coins. He then moved towards Adjovi. But just before he could touch Adjovi again six new children entered the room. They were also coming for some coins. The more he gave them the more the children went to call more friends. Mr Kafui became irritated because he was going to give part of that money to his wife who had travelled for a funeral and would be coming home the next day. He would use the rest as transport fare to Accra, to check his sixteen months salary arrears at the Controller and Accountant General Department.

Unable to cope with the influx of children coming into the room for money, Light Off went for a cane and they all ran away. He therefore gave his bag to Adjovi to bring it to him in his house in the evening. She must come at that time since her friends might have, perhaps, gone to watch T.V in Mr. Dzinyela's house.

44

Just before Kafui stepped out of the room, Fafanyo coughed loudly. Surprised, Kafui turned only to see Fafanyo jump out of the window, showing clean pair of heels. But he ran away through the bush only to come face to face with Awoézo who was busy planting his plantain suckers. Hold-My-Thighs threw away whatever was in his hands. He then picked a cudgel and started chasing the young boy. He threw the weapon at him. The weapon landed on Fafanyo's ankle; and he tripped several times over stumps of trees before falling to the ground.

CHAPTER 9

Two weeks came quickly. After the Wednesday worship had ended, Mr. Otoo-Mensah talked to the entire students. The students listened with rapt, undivided attention because they had waited with bated breath for that morning. They could no longer bear to wait to hear about the information in those three letters. But before he spoke he beckoned to Pious Monyoh Kafui.

They exchanged some whispers and Kafui—who had just preached a soul-touching and an all-inspiring sermon—moved back. He moved to the back of the room where Fafanyo and the rest of the students fond of misbehaving were standing. Kafui made sure that silence had swallowed the giggle and the chuckle and the somewhat noisy gleeful laughter that came from the back of the room at the dying embers of the sermon. It was a big room—two different classrooms whose wooden partition had been removed so that it was used as an Assembly Hall on Wednesdays and on special occasions.

'As you sit and stand in this room you all have missions to fulfill in life. You have visions to realize under the sun. And they all start from today. *The child is the father of the man.* What you'll be in future depends on what you will do today.' He breathed out, touching the bridge of his pointed nose. The obviously stubborn students were quiet. They were now listening and Mr. Otoo-Mensah was impressed about that. By the time he finished driving home his message they would all put away their bad behaviour. He was cocksure.

'If you want to be great in future it all starts from today— be it a doctor, a lawyer, engineer, accountant, newscaster…and what have you. A-and…and a teacher,' he almost forgot about himself—his own profession. 'And anything at all you could imagine in this world. All things are possible. Rome was not built in a day. Today is only a day and by a gradual process we shall all achieve our aims one day if only we attach seriousness to whatever we do today. I promise you.' From every side of the room, there was a spontaneous applause which echoed from the back and hit the ceiling above before bouncing back again to push and stir the soul of the speaker, making him more charged than before.

'But how can we achieve our aims in the future that I'm talking about? It can be done by education. From basic education we can go further to the senior high schools. From there we can go to polytechnics, training colleges and even up to the universities. And everybody shall be rich. And you shall see no poverty. Poverty shall no longer live with your mothers. For this reason you must do your assignments, do every class exercise, take part in every examination, and come to school every day. And never forget to make reading a habit. And one day,'—he beat his chest before hitting the table in front of him—'you shall all agree with me that education is the key to success in life and the bedrock of every country's development. For this reason don't put off what you're supposed to do today for tomorrow. Tomorrow never comes. Tomorrow is the only happy day in the life time of the lazy person. Easy things that should have been done yesterday become the very hard work today. The good book is even telling us that, "If you wait for perfect conditions you will never get anything done".' The students broke into a spontaneous applause. Were they touched?

Minutes later, Mr. Otoo-Mensah's file was brought from his office. The students were happy and ready to listen to him when he picked those three envelopes brought by the postman two weeks ago. (After all that was what they were all waiting for.) He looked at his wrist watch as he opened the letters. It was quarter to nine. Mr. Otoo-Mensah had exceeded his target time. He looked round the assembly hall.

The students giggled as Awoézo approached the direction of Fafanyo. Arms put behind himself, he was nodding and twitching his lips. He wore a black pair of shoes whose mouths were looking to the heavens. He wore a big blue long sleeves shirt over a pair of colonial brown trousers. Like the rest of his pair of trousers, it was very tight at his thighs, between his knees and hips but was baggy and flowing loosely at his lower legs, below his knees and just above his ankles. He had tucked in his shirt and fastened with a yellow belt.

Before Awoézo moved to the other side of the room, Fafanyo screamed lightly. The students around hardly saw how the science teacher nudged Fafanyo with his long thumb nails before intentionally stamping on his sore toe with the heel of his shoe which was sharply cut at an angle of forty-five degrees. He then stroked his moustache.

According to the first letter there was going to be a debate competition among the schools in the district on the motion: *Causes and Effects of Road Accidents in Ghana: The Government, Witches and Wizards must be blamed.* By reason of common sense there was the need for the school to start early preparation since there was going to be fantastic prizes for the winners. There would also be special prizes for participating schools.

In the second letter an N.G.O was bringing assorted books to stock the library of the school. This would take place in the next six days. The third letter was what threw the entire room into wild applause. Flanked by the rest of the teachers,

Mr. Otoo-Mensah called Biba. First, he gave the letter to him. He smiled at him and allowed him to read it aloud in the hearing of every Tom, Dick and Harry.

...Due to your sterling performance about six months ago, the District Education Office has selected your school to represent the district in the Inter-District Drama and Culture Competition to be hosted in Ho. It would take place in the next four months at Ho Social Centre, after the debate competition. Aside the prizes at stake the winning school would also represent the Volta Region in the National Drama and Culture Competition which would take place at the National Theatre in Accra. There would be many important personalities in attendance including the president of the Republic of Ghana. The three boys and the four girls who would emerge as the most talented and promising performers in the Drama competition would be awarded scholarships. The government would see them through all levels of their education... up to the university. The boys would attend Mfantsipim School while the girls would attend Wesley Girls' High School both in Cape Coast or equally good shools around. But the most important thing is that those four girls who would do well in the national drama competition would have the opportunity to visit the United States president in the White House.

It was, indeed, refreshing news for the entire students and staff who screamed and shouted in the room. Should their school do well it would bring glory and honour to the school.

The issue of teachers refusing postings to the village might be a thing of the past.

Having a foreknowledge of the contents of the letters, Mr. Otoo-Mensah and his staff had already met. They had agreed to the former's proposal that a delegation be sent to Winneba to see Dzifa, their colleague teacher who was on a sick leave. Aside being a Catering teacher Dzifa was also a fashion designer and a dramatist; and it was one of the reasons why the headmaster would never release her to a bigger school the third time she applied for leave. Adjovi and her friends would be happy to be in Wesley Girls' one day or visit the U.S.A to see the man that Papa Aganu had told them about some years back before that man finally became the first black president of U.S.A.

CHAPTER 10

It was quarter to six of the clock in the evening. Children hurried to Mr. Dzinyela's house to watch *Captain Planet*, their favourite programme shown on *Nyabrōō T.V.*

On a Saturday like this children from the village trooped to Mr. Dzinyela's house to watch T.V. It was also the time the children were expected to be neat since their feet were critically examined before they were allowed to enter the living room where the television was positioned.

At half past six the programme got started. The children's interest kept soaring higher and higher. They clapped their hands when *Captain Planet*, the hero himself—who only came when his people called on him—appeared from the smoky clouds. As usual he came to rescue his people—who were called the planeteers—from their suffering.

The children drew closer to Aganu. John Sackey later asked the old man whether he could put all his wisdom in his head into a book and sell them so that they could read in schools.

'Knowledge is like a baobab tree. Nobody can wrap his hands around it,' the old man said, stroking his beard and his moustache. He cleared the children's mind about the fact that he was not the only wise person in the world as they had presumed. 'But that notwithstanding—'he stroked his bushy, unkempt hairs—'do you think a human being would use his money to buy wisdom while material things abound?' 'Yes,' the children said together. He chuckled after he was challenged that 'everybody loves wisdom'. Virgin Bingo, Mr. Dzinyela's cat jumped onto Aganu's laps, trying to enter his cloak.

51

'If everybody loves wisdom,' the old man lamented,' then why should a human being, a man who God had given senses and conscience makes his own brother or sister a slave? Why should somebody sit down and think and hope for evil to befall his neigbour? Why should somebody who has a lot of money drive away a poor child? Again why a virgin girl should be made to go to the shrine to suffer for what somebody had done wrong?' Virgin Bingo angrily got down from Aganu's laps when a mouse appeared on the television. The mouse was hiding behind a farm cart and was trying to dodge a cat which had wanted to attack its neck with its sharp claws.

'You're all children,' Aganu said. 'When you grow I'll talk to you in details of what happens in the shrine. I'll make things clearer to you. If you travel beyond the obvious things will become clear to you.' Koku secretly stamped on the toe of one six year old boy, making that boy scream. Aganu left the room and came outside.

Godson asked a bold question after thorough thinking. He wanted to know about why Aganu did not sleep in his room but under a poor shed at the outskirt of the village. But the old man said he was doing that as a form of protest against injustice on the land.

Aganu wanted to explain what he meant by crime and injustice because the children were unable to understand. They could only imagine the issue of their friends who sometimes got drowned in the sea and the lagoon when they went out for fishing and some of their age mates who were pregnant or had given birth. But these issues were not unusual because the children had seen them several times. Had it not been the pressure mounted on him by two older men who had come there he would not have even mentioned *tro-kosi* let alone to discuss it. The reason was that some of the children had their sisters already serving in different shrines and anything could happen to any of them should their fathers or grandfathers die.

'So, Papa Aganu,' Adjovi asked a question. 'Can somebody who would want to get scholarship to a senior high school be taken to the shrine?' Aganu kept quiet. But A.D Olivia almost repeated the question. 'How could somebody who would visit U.S.A on scholarship be taken to the shrine for no reason?' Aganu kept quiet again as he pondered over the question more thoroughly. It was somewhat complicated and unpleasant issue to deal with because it needed carefulness and precision. If he was not careful he would give an erroneous conclusion resulting from awkward reasoning and what he would say would later turn out to be a fallacy of a hasty conclusion.

Aganu wanted to avoid the question. The time for explanation might come by itself. Aside, it was almost nine. He had not eaten since ten in the morning when he ate banku with *Keta school boys* (a kind of tiny fishes from the lagoon.)

'Anyway, what did you say?' He had not forgotten about the question yet he turned to John Sackey, the boy who had asked the first question so that he could be sure of a better answer to give.

'I asked whether you could, please, put all your wisdom or what you have been telling us into a book and sell so that we can read them in schools.'

After careful thought Aganu gave an answer which seemed to summarise all his worries over the injustices on the land. 'I shall sell a book of wisdom for thousand pieces of gold and there will be people who will say that it is cheap.' He gave a broad smile, got up from his seat and picked his sackcloth bag.

'And I shall give a key to understanding it and almost none shall take it even for free.' As he finished talking the children burst into laughter because there were only two teeth left in his mouth.

CHAPTER 11

On Tuesday there was a mini durbar of chiefs. Togbui Amekudzi and his people gathered on the school field. The students dressed in their well-ironed uniform. They listened to solemn renditions from the royal drummers who had come from the palace. Suddenly, a Toyota van hooted persistently blowing dust particles onto the roofs of people's huts. The bus eventually emerged out of the storm-like dust and the students ran to meet it. There was a drawing of a toddler on one side of the van. On the other side one bony old man was carrying many books in a tray on the sides of the bus. Beneath these sketches were boldly written. *'BUY A NEW BOOK AND WEAR AN OLD JACKET'.*

The visitors offloaded assorted books from the van. The books ran into thousands of cedis and so the officers advised the entire school to take good care of them. They then advised the students especially the girls to take their lessons seriously. Next, they promised to come back with computers and more books should the school come out of their two competitions with flying colours.

No sooner had the people left than a new taxi cab surfaced from a distance with top speed. Mr. Otoo-Mensah was happy to see that the other occupant apart from the driver was Dzifa.

John Sackey rang the bell for a morning assembly. Mrs. Mary Dzifa Essuman stood in front of the students who had formed long queues according to their various classes with 'shortest' in front. Her glance fell on Fafanyo. She realised the boy was seriously eyeing her from the back when she turned her bulky back. It was the third time within five minutes.

Kafui got to know about what was happening because he and Awoézo had been monitoring Fafanyo for some days now. Kafui rushed to the back where the boys in Form 3 seemed to be misbehaving. As he took a third step his face changed instantly. He saw that Adjovi was turning to look at a boy who had pulled her dress. 'Foolish girl…' he said. This happened at the very nose of Dzifa yet Dzifa could see nothing. *'A stranger has big eyes but cannot see what happens in town.'* Indeed Dzifa was a stranger in her own country.

The assembly dispersed. The students moved into their various classes. But Awoézo and Kafui were still monitoring every step of Fafanyo. Torsu and Fiagbe joined them because there had been complaints about people's pens and pencils getting missing from their pockets during or right after assembly. Meanwhile, Fafanyo was unaware that he was being monitored with eagle eyes.

Licking and smacking his lips, Fafanyo looked at Dzifa's hips; and how her huge buttocks shook gently from left to right as she was returning to stand in the shade provided by the trees on the school compound.

Fafanyo smiled and smacked again. He intentionally joined the students who moved towards the Form 2 block where Dzifa was panting for breath after answering and talking for a long time with some of the students who had come to greet her. As she turned to respond to a greeting by Innocent, Fafanyo cleverly touched her buttocks. Dzifa felt it. She turned herself. It might be something else. She thought again. The faces of those who passed around her showed that none of them could do such a thing. She thought but she was still not convinced. However, as she stood helpless, shrugging her shoulders with mixed feelings Torsu shook his head. He had seen what had happened. He felt embarrassed about the unfortunate incident. He had seen it all and was still unable to make a head or tail out of Fafanyo's behaviour. People of this nature should be given special attention. He thought. 'We must advise him seriously before he grows. If a young tree starts growing in a wrong direction it must be checked immediately else it cannot be made straight when it grows.'

But Awoézo and Kafui thought otherwise. They rushed towards the direction of the Form 1class, where Fafanyo had passed and was trying to dodge. 'Hey you...hey you...come here, you foolish boy. Good for nothing...come over here.' The students, including Fafanyo himself checked themselves before pointing to one another whether they were the ones being called. 'No,' Hold-My-Thighs and Light Off roared again. 'You...yes you, Fafanyo. Come here. Go and kneel down over there... you naughty boy.' He wanted to run away but was shocked at the mention of his name; and for that matter he remained fixed at where he was. John Sackey went to ring the bell for the first lesson to start.

Even though they had Agricultural Science lesson, there was no teacher in the Form 1class. The master in charge had not been discharged from the hospital following the accident. This was according to reports by Torsu and two other teachers who had visited him some weeks back. The doctor in charge of the emergency ward at the Winneba hospital lamented over the facts that some of the limbs of some of the accident victims would have to be amputated. They were not responding to treatment.

As the students talked about Fafanyo who had knelt down in the sun, Adjovi and two others sneaked out of the class into the library. Godson asked them to wait for him so that they would all go together after he had finished finding out from the headmaster about when they would have a new Agricultural Science teacher. Mr. Otoo-Mensah felt sorry for the students who were missing lessons on how to grow crops and rear animals—the programme the country must seriously look at if it wants to develop. He also bemoaned the fact that most teachers—especially the ladies—posted to the Konkodeka Experimental J.H.S failed to accept postings to the place. They manoeuvered their ways to be reposted to Kpando, Keta, Tema, Takoradi, Kumasi or Accra… and other urban areas where they could get whatever they wanted. 'Such teachers,' Mr. Otoo-Mensah used to say, 'want to avoid suffering in life. Their uncalled-for, their unpatriotic attitudes lead to the neglect of the poor village folks and dearly cause them their future. It's even strange how these same teachers receive The National Best Teachers' Awards at the end of the day at the expense of the village teacher who had sacrificed all his life to shape the future of the poor younger generation.'

Godson was in the reading room—a small room where the students sat silently to read their notes and textbooks. No sooner had he emerged from that place than the school librarian stormed out of the periodicals. The periodicals section was close to the *newspapers section*—where there were a lot of journals and magazines. The journals and magazines were found on a wooden framework with bar hooks for holding things. Adjovi and Godson asked of the name for the wooden structure and the man said, '*racks*'.

'Good morning, Sir.'

'Good morning. How are you?' The librarian put his left arm on Adjovi's shoulders and his right on Godson's. 'What can I do for you, a lady and a gentleman?'

'We're looking for *Philosophy of Rabbi The Unknown Servant.* We've tried every means yet we cannot locate it.' John Sackey chanced upon a pocket-sized book. At the back was written *History and Adventures of Asebu Amenfi.* He picked the book and skimmed through. Nodding, he looked at the title of it for the third time. He imagined how the author, Obed Acquah Quansah, had managed to write such a fascinating book.

'Well,' the librarian said. 'If you cannot remember the one who wrote the book you can still go to the author's catalogue.'

'Author's catalogue?' The name sounded strange. 'Uh, what is that? Where is it?'

The librarian pointed his finger at where the Senior Girls' Prefect had put one leg across the other while reading the *'Daily Graphic'.* There was some noise outside and so the girl vacated her seat and left. 'Waow...'Adjovi whispered beckoning to Godson and the two others. She had seen another newspaper, *'Ghanaian Times'* which would help them greatly to win the contest over their seniors. That was why both the old man and their headmaster had been asking them to make reading a habit. They said among themselves. That newspaper was a Wednesday edition. On the front page, under the banner headline was a picture of a mangled 207 Benz bus which plied between Takoradi and Accra. It was rare to find such a picture. The bus was beyond repairs and had to be disposed off as scrap since it was only fit for making coal pots.

Beside the bus, a pregnant woman had died in a pool of blood. She was now being taken on a stretcher into an ambulance. From how the reporter, Emmanuel Halm, carried the news item only ten out of the thirty three passengers had survived with varying degrees of injury.

According to an eye witness' report the bus had plenty items loaded on its carrier. The vehicle was on top speed when it suddenly came face to face with a tipper truck which had been parked on the road side. The driver negotiated a sharp curve which made the bus hit the truck and somersaulting several times into a nearby bush. After the accident, the paper reported, a half bottle of gin was found under the driver's seat when the victims were being retrieved from the mangled bus. Adjovi and her mates had got a good point. Both the driver's licence and the road- worthy certificate had expired two years before; and it was therefore strange how the police at various barriers and vantage positions failed to detect anything of that sort. The motion for the debate quickly flashed through the minds of the students again. *Causes and Effects of Road Accidents in Ghana: The Government, Witches and Wizards must be blamed.* They would be ready whether to speak *for* or *against* the motion. They read on. Meanwhile, the students screamed from inside their classrooms because Hold-My-Thighs had picked a big cane to flog Fafanyo. Within a split second the assembly ground had become full with anxious eyes to see what was really happening.

CHAPTER 12

Fafanyo proved difficult. Four strong boys from Form 3 were therefore called upon to overpower him. Kafui brought a table and they stretched him on it. Quickly, Awoézo rushed to the office and brought a big cane saying, '*Afi du ke, ke mevona le efe nkume o.* (The mouse that eats a jute bag will always remember to eat others.) I want to tell you that a bad habit starts early and remains forever. He added angrily, 'Look at your face...*like figures written on the face of a pink sheet...*'

Fafanyo begged Dzifa's mercy. 'I beg you Madam,' he sobbed, his eyes now as red as the eyes of a cat which had been hit against a wall. But Awoézo would not listen to any plea. He twisted his lips and faced the students. 'Today your friend is in trouble. Tomorrow it may be your turn. We are coming to exorcise *the spirit of Suarez* from this boy so that he can no longer have the teeth to bite innocent men.' He stroked his moustache. 'He will also not have the hands to pull away balls from entering his father's goal post let alone having the dirty hands to touch the 'vital statistics' of adorable women again.'

However, Mr. Otoo-Mensah decided to have a five-minute meeting in his office with the rest of the teachers to decide the fate of the boy as Dzifa herself felt pity for him even though Fafanyo had been rude to her.

'So what do we do?' Mr. Otoo-Mensah turned to Biba. 'Ee...eh,' Biba hardly had anything to say. As an assistant Guidance and Counseling Coordinator he had started talking to Fafanyo three days before and hoped that the boy would turn over a new leaf. He also feared that if Fafanyo was sacked from the school the boy's future might be impaired.

'But I sometimes blame his mother, Daavi So-fire. I'll also accuse Efo Nikanika, his father who due to his accident has stopped fishing and is now operating a corn mill.' Anytime Fafanyo was punished Daavi So-fire would insult and fight the teacher who punished her son. And she was too careless to go to the extent of using her long nails to fight the teacher concerned at the market or in the street or in the alley or in any available space. She had once come to the school to fight Torsu and some few other teachers.

Kafui—the headmaster's most trusted and respected colleague—strongly protested what his assistant, Biba was suggesting. '*Agbebada nōta kubada wo kuna*' (Those who do bad things, also die in bad ways.) If our elders say this, then why should Fafanyo be spared for the last time? He should never be allowed to go scot-free. Surely he must face the music. Somebody shouted *Abraham Lincoln* from the back of the crowd; and Kafui went wild. Mr. Otoo-Mensah complained about why Nikanika had not been advising his wife to give up her behaviour. The *seniors* and the four strong boys still surrounded Fafanyo. But the rest of the students chanted for their friend Fafanyo who was now in hot waters.

'Sir,' the Maths teacher, Fiagbe Fiawomom, raised his hand. He was coming to say something. This man was so surprised at how Fafanyo was able to top the entire class in mathematics, when he had eighty five percent. Upon further investigations he came to believe that he stole Godson's paper. When the examination papers were being collected Fafanyo quickly pulled Godson's paper at the blind side of the invigilator. He cancelled Godson's name and wrote his own name on it. He then cancelled his own name on his paper and wrote Godson's name on it. (This happened when he saw that

Godson had finished long ago and had turned himself to teach somebody.) Before Godson realised, the papers had been collected. Fiagbe was also unable to detect what Fafanyo had done during marking.

'S-sir, I... I ha... ha... have-ve s-something to say...'Innocent walked towards the maths teacher, into the office with his exercise book. There was a question that everybody was marked right except him. He was unable to bear the laughter and taunts from Olivia and other classmates including Joycelyn and Hilda. Getting those marks back would help him get nine out of a maximum of twenty marks. But the teacher quickly frowned at him. He gnashed his teeth and twisted his lips before raising a blow. Innocent quickly ran back with a sad face. Meanwhile, the students kept chanting and cheering Fafanyo's name. Adjovi, Godson and John Sackey came to stand at the entrance of the library for some time before returning to continue with their reading.

The librarian took Adjovi and Godson to the author's catalogue. It was found in a filing cabinet which had in it card index of all authors whose works were in the library. He then asked them to check all the drawers. Luckily, they found out the book was available in the library when Adjovi pulled the third drawer but did not know where exactly it could be found. The librarian then directed them to check out from the second shelf which stood behind them.

'Sir, please can you give it to us?' They said when their hands eventually touched the book. 'We want to borrow it.'

The librarian looked inside their hands. 'Why not? Anyway, do you have your library membership cards on you?'

They looked at the librarian's face. They were almost new comers in the library. The man, however, handed them over to one of the library assistants who asked for their particulars before issuing them with library membership cards. This would give them the chance to borrow books home and return them at the appropriate date. The book in their hands, the woman said, could not be taken home. They argued with her because the librarian had told them that once they had the cards they could borrow any book they wanted. The librarian explained to them. 'All books may be borrowed but some are for *reference only.* This means they cannot be taken out of the library.' From outside, the students kept chanting Fafanyo's name. Adjovi, Godson and John Sackey rushed out of the library.

Still, Mr. Otoo-Mensah's question about Efo Nikanika received no response. Torsu lived just a stone's throw from where the man operated his corn mill machine where he obtained milled maize for his fowls. He had this to say:

'Fafanyo's parents live in one room with their seven children who are all grownups. And in the night they might hear what happens… I hope you've gotten what I'm talking about.'

Dzifa nodded by this revelation. She had heard a secret. That might account for the boy's behaviour. Mr. Otoo-Mensah now remembered having overheard from the children's conversation that Fafanyo had once told them he sometimes watched *video* in their room at midnight. And it was true. When Efo Nikanika found out that his children were fast asleep he would put out the lantern and move closer to Daavi So-fire, her wife. By that time Fafanyo who would not be asleep saw whatever his parents were doing.

'One Friday,' Torsu continued. 'Daavi So-fire travelled for a funeral. There was also another funeral here in Konkodeka. Efo Nikanika went and brought in another woman, Daavi Oboshie when all his children had gone to the wake-keeping. But unfortunately Fafanyo was hiding under a pile of unwashed clothes and everything happened in his presence. Early next morning, Nikanika gave him five cedis and promised to buy two canoes for him when he completed school.'

CHAPTER 13

As soon as Dzifa entered the big room the students started talking. They butted and whispered into one another's ears. The words moved and spread through the students. 'Madam ooo... Madam... Madam ooo... Madam...,' they chanted. They then burst into a spontaneous applause; and Dzifa was unable to stop shaking her head and smiling as she walked gallantly towards her seat for things to start. She knew it was because of her special appearance that day which had, perhaps, thrown her students into jubilation.

Dzifa was flanked by the rest of the teachers. She sat in front of the competitors who were seated in a semi-circle. She gasped with relief before picking out a white cotton handkerchief from her bluish bag—a colour that matched perfectly with her apparel and her moccasin that housed her smooth spotless feet. She bowed her head a bit behind the table in front of her and blew her nose so softly that those around her were unable to hear. She did this to show the spectacle that she might have seen but the students cheered and screamed at whatever she did. 'These children will kill me,' she shook her head again as she picked a pen and used the top cover to scratch through her hair which had been plaited into long braids and wound into a crown on top of her head. Next, she shoved back her chair, giving swipes at the corners of her mouth with her handkerchief before tossing it back into the wallet.

It was thirty minutes late, beyond the actual time that the competition should have started. But it was intentional. Dzifa intentionally allowed those minutes so that she could calm nerves. She made the competitors—those who were nervous—

feel relaxed because they had not sat in front of a big audience like that before. She greeted the students and said one or two things. Innocent got up to clean the chalkboard for the score master to use. The time keeper, Fiagbe, sounded the bell and the competition started.

It was an educative and thought-provoking exercise where the students cracked their brains to do their best. Impressed by the mental agility of the contestants, Dzifa encouraged the audience to cheer the contestants.

Adjovi wiped the beads of sweats that had formed semi-circle on her forehead with her handkerchief as she contemplated on the point she would use to counter some valid points raised by Jedidiah, the second speaker, an opponent, from the Form 3 class.

Meanwhile, some of the students chanted: 'Fafa ooo... Fafanyo... Fafa ooo... Fafanyo...' Kafui and Awoézo looked through to the back of the room—where the bad boys had gathered—in order to be sure whether Fafanyo was truly in the room because he had been absent for some days now. But there was no Fafanyo. Perhaps the students were joking. After Awoézo had threatened the students to reduce the noise in the room, Dzifa allowed Adjovi to give her last submission after Godson and John Sackey had done their best to maintain the pace. She stood up and mesmerised her fellow students and the panel of judges with cogent points. She was bold and fearless. She was not distracted by the cat calls.

'Mr. Chairman, Panel of judges, Accurate Time Keeper, Fellow Debaters, Ladies and Gentlemen. I'm happy one more time for being put forward by my class teachers and my mates to speak against the motion that *Causes and Effects of Road*

Accidents in Ghana: The Government, Witches and Wizards must be blamed. First of all, I must confess that it's a feather in my cup.' Adjovi spoke with confidence.

'My opponent, Jedidiah, just mentioned the fact that there have been cases of witches and wizards causing road accidents in many villages and on the trunk roads in the country. Among other things, my opponent from Form 3 class said, witches and wizards can cause drivers to continue chatting with women who come and sit beside them on the front seats of their vehicles. This in most cases lead to road accident.' She smiled and shook her head and turned back to face the audience.

'I'm an African and so I cannot disprove this fact. But I'll want my opponent to be aware that this fact is yet to be proved in any court of law. And so this argument will not stand until the day that it will be proven in a spiritual court of law where cases involving spiritualism will be heard. Ah! I cannot stand here today and sheepishly watch my opponents especially Jedidiah throw dust in your eyes. He Jedidiah is saying that the government must provide good roads, punish the offenders and officers whose negligence lead to road accidents in the country. It is true all right. But saying that the individuals must not be blamed is where my problem lies.' Both the students and their teachers clapped for Adjovi, the speaker. But the noise about Fafanyo started coming again. He was now with his father and they were heading towards the school.

'Mr. Chairman, I'll want to say emphatically here that my opponent does not know what he is really talking about and so he should give us a break.' She produced four different newspapers she and her colleagues had picked from the library. The papers had in them pictures of serious accidents on the front pages. She showed them one after the other to the students before turning to show them to the teachers. Next, she frowned and threw her hands in the air.

'Are my opponents saying that we should blame the government, witches, wizards and other spirits instead of the individuals such as the drivers themselves? If they say so then, Mr. Chairman, excuse my saying that my opponents are living in a fool's paradise. Are they also saying that we should not blame those who get drunk before coming to sit in front of the steering wheels? That we should not blame those passengers who want to get home early and as a result put pressure on some already confused drivers to go beyond expected speed limits and thereby making unnecessary overtaking?' Adjovi wiped away sweat from her face and continued:

'Are people saying that we should not blame the policemen who regularly collect bribes from offending drivers and allow them to go scot-free? That we should not blame the officers at the Drivers' and Vehicle Licensing Authority (D.V.L.A) who collect huge sums of money from individuals and give them driving licence even though they can neither read nor identify road signs or lack the basic science of driving and...?

'These officers are paid by the state or the government. And if by their bad attitudes people are disabled or die shouldn't we put the blame on them? Shoudn't we single them out and hold them responsible for their negligence and omissions but rather shift blames to the door step of the government who has many other pressing issues to bother about them? One-third of the students clapped thunderously. However, the rest screamed uncontrollably. Efo Nikanika had reached the door with two machetes in his hands.

CHAPTER 14

Some students started jumping through the windows. They jumped as fast as their feet could carry them. The headmaster as well as the teachers joined the race. This caused fighting and stampede and some of them fell and got hurt. In fact, it was strange. As the teachers fought for their own lives they left behind the students who needed protection. They had run for their dear lives. Safety first, they say.

His face darkened with fury, Efo Nikanika entered the room with his machetes. He was ready to harm anybody who dared to stop him. The school children cried from outside because Dzifa was yet to escape from the room. As Efo Nikanika dangled the two machetes in the air Dzifa's heart pounded faster and abnormally.

'Where is that *Hold-My-Thighs*?' Efo Nikanika yelled. One teacher passed by the window and so the man asked again, rushing on him. 'Are you Hold-My-Thighs?' anger had made him forget that he and Torsu stayed in the same area. But Fafanyo rushed to his father, begging. *'It is not called* Hold-My-Thighs. *It is called Mr. Torsu. Papa, leave him alone.'* An angry Nikanika obeyed his dearest son. But he tapped Torsu's back softly with the handle of a machete before allowing him to go. He then screamed, gnashing his teeth.

'I want H-ho-l-ld-My-Thighs... I want H-ho-l-ld-My-Thighs... 'I want H-ho-l-ld-my-...' He screamed as he gave out his weapon to Fafanyo so that he could adjust his cloth that seemed to be falling off his waist. He then removed the towel that hang on his shoulder, wiped his face with it before asking for chewing stick from Fafanyo who pulled three from his pocket. That might equally cool his anger if there was no water. His anger was bad for his own liking.

Fafanyo pointed to Kafui. 'That teacher are one of them.' Efo Nikanika's body started to shake as he needed more clarification from his son. 'You are sure?' he asked. Fafanyo replied. 'Am sure, Papa,' he cried, saying something that every teacher would never agree. 'This teacher like my girl. He like *my girl* and so he always hate me?' But Pious Monyoh-Kafui talked out of fear, his voice trailing off. 'Me I like your girl?' He spat to the floor. 'May God forbid!'

Efo raised his machete, asking, 'So this is Mr. Light Off? 'Yes,' Fafanyo cried. 'He is also called *Abraham Lincoln.* He will do Science experiments right now.'

'You call me *"Mr. Light off"* in my presence... and *Abraham Lincoln,* too?' Kafui was taking aback yet he behaved wisely. He talked no more. 'It is foolhardiness for a person to argue with a man holding a gun or a sharp machete.'

Efo Nikanika did not spare him. He hit his shoulders with the back of his machete before punching his nose with his fist. People rushed to the J.H.S block.

Mr. Otoo-Mensah felt sorry for the shouting and screaming that had plunged his peaceful school into confusion. But didn't he foresee that happening? Yes he did. He foresaw that happening from the way the two teachers handled Fafanyo. His basic knowledge in Psychology reminded him that an angry teacher should not punish a child. Remembering this, he tried to save the poor boy when he realised that the two teachers were angry. For Kafui, Mr. Otoo-Mensah knew it was because he wanted to help the boy have a good future and that was the only reason he supported him to discipline Fafanyo that way. For Awoézo, Mr. Otoo-Mensah quite remembered ever receiving complaints from him, about Fafanyo and few other students who had not been allowing his crops to grow. He had suspected those recalcitrant students of stealing his pear, mango, banana, maize and other crops from his garden.

Fafanyo wore nothing on top. Marks of canes and tiny bruises could be seen on his back even from afar. How Awoézo and Kafui beat him that day worried Mr. Otoo-Mensah. But that did not mean the headmaster supported the argument that because of 'child rights' a student must not be disciplined or caned when that person has done something wrong. After warning a student three times, he believed that the next thing to follow was punishment to correct him or deter others from copying his behaviour; and this principle had helped improve the level of discipline in the school. However, he feared for the consequences of Awoézo's action. He feared that should the District Education Office get to know about that the Science teacher or he, the headmaster himself might be in trouble. But then he took consolation in the fact that the people of the village knew nothing about their rights let alone to report a teacher for subjecting their children to severe beatings.

Miss Emma Spio-Dotse and Miss Esi Motey went on their knees. They begged Efo Nikanika to drop the machete in his hands. Meanwhile, Daavi So-fire appeared from behind with four pieces of canes. One boy signalled to Fafanyo. He hinted that Hold-My-Thighs was hiding under a table in the headmaster's office. Quickly, an angry Fafanyo told his father.

But Mr. Otoo-Mensah pleaded and pleaded until he agreed to drop his weapons so that Awoézo would come out from his hideout.

'What do you think you can do? Do you know what your son did to Dzifa? How he wanted to disgrace our beautiful Madam?'

'You sure?'

'Yes.'

'You say you are sure? Then call Dzifa here?'

'N-no... Yes,'Awoézo replied with feigned courage. He took two steps backwards. 'Fafanyo is also a thief. He and his friends always steal my maize and mangoes?'

'You mean Fafanyo my son? You mean Fafanyo my best child who is always first in class? I cannot believe you.' Efo wept saying, '*Ekpōe* (You will see). Do you think my son Fafanyo is a child who would lie?' He was now fuming with rage. He bowed to pick a stone to throw at Awoézo. *'It is also called Single Spine. And that is his botanical name,'* Fafa cried. the crowd had increased greatly.

However, Efo saw the bruises at the back of his son and so he cried: '*Oh dear Fafa... Oh dear Fafanyo my son... Fafanyo my son...*' The students burst into laughter when he said this. Disturbed by the situation, Mr Otoo-Mensah had to intervene. But Fafanyoh's father frowned at him. 'You *Judas...*'

'M-me...' Mr. Otoo-Mensah shook his head. 'You call me Judas?'

'Yes, you told the teachers to kill my son.'

'Please... D-don't. Don't...'

'Shut... Shut up... Sh-shut up...' Efo panted while sweating. 'You *Judas-is-Carrot.* Leave my son alone. Go to Jaasikan, your hometown and tell people to beat their children.'

'You said I am Judas is wh-hat?'

'*Judas-is-Carrot.*' Efo and his wife, So-fire shouted together. 'Didn't you hear?' So-fire added, rushing towards the head of the school.

Mr Otoo said it in his head, 'Judas is pineapple; not Judas is Carrot.'

Still, Hilda and Joycelyn Tetteh screamed. Olivia, Lois, and the rest of the students jubilated. Being his best moment, Innocent joined the K.G children who had come around the scene. They clapped their hands in admiration whereas John Sackey intermittently rang the bell to control the piercing noise. That was when Daavi So-fire rushed on Eyram (a.k.a *Mama Leave-My-Legs*), Awoézo's wife. As tiny as she was So-fire threw herself onto Eyram, a respectable woman, and the two started to fight. They tumbled, turned and turned each other in the dust while the children cheered and applauded.

CHAPTER 15

Adjovi slept and had a dream. She dreamt that a man with a long beard and protruding stomach was chasing her. She therefore ran to climb a coconut tree. On the top of the tree was a python. At the base was also a lion waiting to devour her. She cried and shouted. The sound of her voice now disturbed her two elder sisters to wake up. 'What's wrong, Adjo? What's wrong with you today too? The two of us are with you here. Tell us something. Are you alright?' They rushed to their mother's room, complaining about how Adjovi was panting and how her garment was soaked with sweat.

In the morning Adjovi looked dejected. She sat behind their hut, still confused. It was the third time she had had such a terrible dream. 'Instead of being chased by an old man calling me "my wife...my wife" why didn't I dream that I was in an aeroplane? Why didn't I dream that I was flying to America to visit the White House? Why didn't I dream that I had been crowned the best of all the debaters who would be meeting at Keta next week to compete? Why wasn't I selected as the most talented performer in the debate competition?' Smiling, Koku walked towards her. 'That snake must be a witch or a wizard.' Adjovi continued talking as she looked at her palms. There were scars of healed cuts—cuts she had sustained from breaking and cracking stones into small pieces during weekends and vacation and on holidays.

'Why didn't I see gold on that tree? Why didn't all the fruits up there turn into gold for me? I would have been richer. I would have got money to take Papa to the hospital at Keta.' She shook her head. 'I would have also stopped going to the hill side to break stones at dawn, before and after school.'

'Adjo, my mother says I should come and call you,' Koku said. 'Are you coming with me?' He coughed.

'And if I hadn't opened my eyes the lion would have torn me apart, breaking all my bones. No'—she argued with herself—'I would have mentioned the name of Jesus three times. Jesus... Jesus... Jesus...' Koku patted her shoulders. He wanted to knock her head.

'Ah, Koku, is that you?' Adjovi came back to herself.

'I've been standing here for more than five minutes.' Koku cried.

'E...eh'

'Yes,' Koku looked back. Adjovi's friends were coming from afar with buckets and pots.

'Are you sure?' Adjovi wondered.

'Oh. I don't lie.' Koku dipped his finger into the soil, looked above and licked it. This meant he was saying nothing but the truth.

'And why didn't... And why didn't I want to one day be in the university. I want to be awarded a scholarship. How could Adjovi be in the shrine? Why didn't you call me?' Her thoughts were incoherent.

'Uh,' Koku was surprised that after Adjo had finished talking to herself she was lost in that short conversation, too. 'Are you alright, Adjo?'

'I'm alright, Koku? Nothing is wrong with me,' she forced a smile while scratching through her hair to allow some air to blow through.

'But why were you talking all alone to yourself? A-are ...are you m-m-a...are you *m-married*? Actually he wanted to ask whether she was getting mad, but quickly changed the statement.

'Can a child like me marry?'

Koku laughed loudly. 'My mother says I should come and call you.'

'I'm sorry,' Adjovi cupped her mouth with her hand. Eyram told her yesterday to come and help her wash some clothes but had long forgotten. Awoézo's wife had still not recovered from the pains she sustained when Daavi So-fire came to fight her in the school some days back. That tiny, slender woman had used her long, sharp nails to scratch her neck, cheeks and face. But Eyram was quite lucky. The reason was that in all her fights, Daavi So-fire used broken bottles as well as any implement she might get hold of. She used her teeth as well. For that matter other women feared going near her husband.

'Go and tell Aunte Eyram that I'm coming,' Adjovi said. She would not go but she remembered something. *Migoto miadzi lawo* (Obey your parents). She still thought about going back to the hillside to break some stones since it was a Saturday. After buying new uniforms, she would use the money gained to buy for herself some yoghurt. How sweet it would taste looking at how the small boys and girls enjoyed eating them as they appeared on Mr. Dzinyela's television set, as they appeared on *Nyabrōō TV*.

As they walked home to Eyram's hut, Olivia, Hilda and Joycelyn ran to them. Together, the children looked at some hawks displaying in the air. The birds circled one another in the air. They soared high while their wings were held motionless. They suspended in the sky. They then dived sharply downwards before climbing up gain. It was nice and pleasing to the eyes of the young boys and girls who clapped for the exploits of the birds of prey. They put their pots aside and then watched how the hawks were displaying their aerial agility.

'I wish I had wings,' Hilda said, jumping up and down. 'If I get wings I will go to America just tomorrow.' Adjovi added. 'Me, too…' Godson continued and they all laughed together. 'I'll not go to America. I'll rather go and see mountain Afadjato. Next, I'll go to Cape Coast with Bingo. The two of us will visit the Castle and the Kakum National Park… and then come back later to Kwahu mountains in Easter time. I'll then take the bull by the horn and take part in the Kwahu paragliding exercise.'

The children clapped for them. Meanwhile, as Adjovi's friends picked their pots to the well Innocent ran desperately to their side. He was shouting and screaming. He was running away from the beating of his mother. His back, cheeks and head were oozing with blood.

CHAPTER 16

It was after a Sunday school class when Sister Saviour moved closer to Adjovi who had kept quiet throughout the service.

'Adjo,' she wrapped her arm around the young lady's neck, feeling her body temperature. 'Are you alright?'

'Yes Madam.'

'Has anybody beaten you?'

'No, Madam.'

'But why? Why are you so quiet today? Tell me something, my dear daughter.' They walked through the isle to sit on one of the pews close to the altar where Pastor Nigel Sean Ben-Acquaah stood to utter some words which might alter Adjovi's mood. 'Has Kafui attempted to touch your breasts again?'

She kept quiet. They talked for almost an hour. Later, Sister Saviour handed her over to Pastor Nigel Sean Ben-Acquaah, the overseer of the Quick Prosperity Miracle Church.

Initially, the pastor asked her whether she ate heavily before going to bed. She said 'no'. Even if she had eaten heavily or too late into the night she would make sure, as Awoézo had told them, she would have walked around for some time before going to bed. This would save her from a lot of discomfort the following day. Later, Adjovi talked about her dream and the things she had seen which had made her uncomfortable. But Pastor Nigel advised her to forget about all her fears since it was not the first time she had complained of such a dream. Athough there seemed to be danger ahead the Lord was still on her side and nothing could destroy God's love for her. The man of God assured her. (They would organise a two-day fasting and prayers for her but the Pastor's wife who disliked fasting might secretly eat fufu and palm nut soup.)

'But Pastor,' Adjovi complained. 'I don't understand if you say there might be danger ahead. I'm part of the debaters and all my teachers and friends say and believe that I'll do well. I'm also part of the school drama group and after the debate competition we're going to perform in the inter-district competition which would take place next term at the Ho Social Centre. Madam Dzifa says we shall perform *Romeo and Juliet*. Godson is Romeo and I'm Juliet. If I do well at Ho we'll go to Accra. If I do well there, too I will go to U.S.A.'

Pastor Nigel nodded and smiled. He was happy for Adjovi's growing confidence. 'You'll win both competitions because of your confidence. But you must read your bible and pray everyday. The name of Christ crosses all crises.'

From church Adjovi didn't go home to change her dress. Her New Testament trapped under her armpit, she went straight to Dzifa's hut. But Sammy (or Joe Diggy—a name his friends in class five had coined from his other name, de-Graft Johnson) told her that his mother was not around. The headmaster had come to call her and the two had gone to visit Innocent.

Mr Otoo-Mensah went to Innocent's house with Dzifa. The headmaster held Inoocent's arm, looked at his cheeks and the head. 'This is serious. And so what happened? Innocent wanted to talk. But his mother angrily twisted her lips and gnashed her teeth at him. He kept quiet at once and left the place. In spite of this, Mr. Otoo-Mensah was quick to detect that there was a foul play. There was something wrong somewhere looking at the cuts in Innocent's head; the marks on his back; and the bruises and blisters on his cheeks.

'So Madam,' Mr. Otoo-Mensah asked, almost crying. 'Why do you do this to your own son, eh?'

'What have I done?' Innocent's mother, Efo Agbenaza's wife, asked. 'What have I done to him? Have I killed him?'

'Yes. Yes, you've killed him,' Mr. Otoo-Mensah gradually lost his temper. 'Don't you know that you've almost killed this poor boy?'

The woman got up from her stool. 'Are you the one who buys food for him? Tell me. Tell me, Mr. Headmaster.'

'I'm disappointed in you. I'm so disappointed in you that I'm even lost for words.' He picked his handkerchief from his back pocket and wiped his face. 'I least expected you to do this.' Was he mistaken? Clearly the woman was regarded by many as an angel. At market places she smiled to people and her words were sweeter than honey. When she sang at church, her voice softened the hearts of hardcore criminals and sent the entire congregation straight into the heavens, right before the throne of the Most High.

'Do I care if you're disappointed in me,' Efo Agbenaza's wife looked at the headmaster with an evil look. 'It is God who will judge me... not you.' She set off a quarrel with him.

'I beg you, Madam. May this be your first and last else we shall hand you over to the police. And if you're not lucky you'll be put behind bars.'

'Did I get you right?' The woman's voice started to reduce in its harshness. 'If the police from Keta come I'll tell them what had happened before I did that—'she sneezed—'No. before I did what you people are saying I did to him. Master, I respect you a lot, and I don't want to insult you.'

'Uh.What did I hear you say, Madam? You said you'll insult me? Remember! A cripple never starts a war song. You don't understand the consequences of what you're saying.'

The woman turned to look at Dzifa who was shocked at how the woman was behaving. 'Have you people asked Innocent about the person who stole my two cedis?'

'I'm not sure Innocent would steal your money. And even if he had done that,' Mr. Otoo-Mensah cried, 'is what you did the required punishment for a boy like Innocent?' He shook his head. 'How much is the worth of two cedis?'

'Are you the one to tell me how to behave, Master?' She stood akimbo, arms folded. 'Allow me to scratch my skin.'

'Uh,' Mr. Otoo-Mensah opened his mouth wide. 'Well, how do you even know it was Innocent who stole that two cedis you're talking about? I can see four other boys and two girls around.' He counted the children who entered and left the woman's single room.

The woman laughed, clapping her hands. She then called six other children so that they came to surround her. 'Do you think a son or a daughter of mine would ever steal? The arguments continued. However, Mrs. Mary Dzifa Essuman asked Mr. Otoo-Mensah that they should leave. People had started coming there one by one, asking of what was happening; and she, being a native of the area, knew what could happen after that.

On their way to their various huts they met Adjovi who was tired of waiting for Dzifa in her house and was now returning home. She asked several times whether her name had been dropped or she was not going to take part in the debate which would take place in the course of the week. Dzifa calmed her fears saying, 'Hope for nothing but the best. You are already in the team. In fact, you've been awarded the scholarship.' She went home with her and gave her some food to eat just to calm her anxiety.

CHAPTER 17

Godson carried forward the old man's stool. His father had instructed him to do so every Sunday, Wednesday and Friday evening when they were coming to listen to stories. Meanwhile, the evening's version of the stories would lose its usual taste. One reason was that two girls from class six were dragged to the shrine to go and worship in one of the shrines around. Another was a young boy in Class 3 who had drowned in the sea when he went on a fishing expedition with his father.

But the most current issue that would take major part in the discussion before the actual story-telling was what had happened to Innocent who was a good friend of the old man. Passionate discussions about how Efo Agbenaza's wife treated Innocent would make the people—especially her colleagues—lose appetite for meals for four days.

'We stand on the shores of bondage and see millions of our people struggling desperately to come out of the sea. But humankind is powerless and weaker vessels to offer them those hands of support!' Aganu cried and the people shook their heads in sorrows. Before the story started Godson was asked to tell a story which was told two months ago. Godson came to stand behind his master, Aganu and told the story as exactly as the old man would have done. Everybody clapped for the young boy. His father, Mr. Bernard Dzinyela's mouth was full of joy and laughter as his own colleagues tapped and praised him for what his son had done.

'One day a farmer went out to farm to inspect a nest of a goose,' Aganu eventually started the story. 'There he realised that the goose—a large water bird with long neck—had laid an egg. He looked at it carefully and he realised that the egg was yellow and it reflected light in glittering flashes. The farmer decided to throw the egg away because he thought a trick had been played on him by the naughty boys around. But he took it up. It was as heavy as lead. He then changed his mind and took it home. Soon he found out that it was not an ordinary egg; it was rather an egg of pure gold.' The crowd clapped their hands, nodding and looking at one another's faces. Aganu got up from his stool and limped over his walking stick towards where Fafanyo had pulled his seat to the side of Adjovi who sat beside Joe Diggy and her mother, Dzifa. Frogs croaked.

As Aganu opened his mouth to continue, somebody—who was still not satisfied with the little discussion done so far on the issue of *tro-kosi*—raised his hand to ask a question. 'Papa Aganu, the person bowed, in full respect. 'You promised to tell us a story of a *tro-kosi* girl who made a journey to the shrine at the time that you were young and were going to school with your classmates, about how that girl fought and killed the priest and his guards who watched over the shrine.'

Aganu kept quiet. He didn't want to respond even though he had promised them a week before that he would use that Sunday evening to throw more light on the *tro-kosi* so that the young boys and girls would be able to know what was happening around them. He pleaded with them. He assured that person to wait for the next week. He was unwilling to tackle the issue that moment because his friends—the school children— would be going for their debate competition on Thursday. The children had prepared so well that the old man thought it unwise to tell them stories that would sadden their hearts. Some of them also had sisters who were still serving in various shrines for the sins of their dead relatives.

'And so what happened next?' The crowd asked when they realised that Aganu, their teacher, was not ready to throw more light on *tro-kosi* or the virgins who were sent to the shrine as slaves to the gods almost throughout their lives. Aganu coughed as he picked dry sticks from the ground. He put them into the fire and stoked it so that the burning firewood gave more light to the place. He then resumed his seat and continued:

'Yes, the farmer found out that the egg was pure gold. And every morning the same thing happened... The goose laid a golden egg every morning. Very soon the farmer became rich through the sale of the golden eggs.' He coughed again. 'However, as the farmer grew richer and richer he became greedier and greedier. He therefore decided or thought to get whatever is in the belly of the goose.' Aganu paused. He threw a rhetorical question to the attentive crowd.

'And how could he get the eggs? Hmmn!' He breathed out heavily, scratching the back of his neck where a mosquito had bitten. 'The man eventually killed the goose. He opened the belly of his goose that laid the golden eggs for him with a knife. However, he found nothing there but faeces and intestines.' The crowd could hardly stop nodding their heads and clapping their hands. Aganu then advised them not to take after that greedy farmer.

'Look out in your quest of making wealth. Anybody who is not happy with what he has would not be content even if the whole world is given to him. Avoid greed and any form of greedy behaviour. Love simplicity. Go your own pace. Don't play to the gallery. Avoid selfishness. No matter what you have you must consider yourself to be lucky and rich. Take your time to grow richer and you shall live the richest. All the pains and troubles in the world come from greed. Avoid being greedy and the world shall be a nice, peaceful place for all of us to live in...' He laughed as the people started leaving the place for their various homes. '... And I also wish all my friends and school children a happy and successful debate on Thursday.'

The school closed early on Wednesday because of the next day's debate. The children went to the well to wash their uniforms and a few clothes they would use for those three days.

Adjovi, Hilda, Olivia and Joycelyn were all part of the drama group. Later in the day, they visited Godson and his sister, Lois. It was interesting and wonderful how the two had neatly ironed their new uniforms and placed them on a hanger. Hunger and anger of their father would vanish should he be tempted to look at how their brown and yellow uniforms had been hanged over the triangular metal frame in their living room. 'I'm going to bring my uniform to iron,' Adjovi said, changing her decision to pull a surprise the following day.' After carefully combining her studies with water-fetching and stone-cracking she had been able to raise some money and had given out fifteen cedis to get a new school uniform.

When Adjovi came home her mother had not returned from farm. She entered her mother's room to take her new uniform. But she was unable to locate it. She rather chanced upon a new big dark cloth.

She went and roamed throughout the farm without seeing her. She then remembered her dream and being scared by her own shadows she ran quickly back home only to see that her mother had passed a different route back home and had started cooking.

'What's wrong with you, Adjo?' Her mother asked her, stopping the palm nut she was pounding. 'Has Kafui done anything to you again? Has he touched your breasts?'

'Fofo, where is my uniform? Adjovi cried. 'Where is my school uniform? Tomorrow is the time for our debate at Keta.'

'Your uniform? Your school uniform?'

'Uh?' Adjo's eyes almost popped out of their sockets. Was she dreaming? 'Fofo, my uniform. I mean my uniform that I gave you money to buy for me a week ago when you said you were travelling to Keta to accompany your friend to bury her father.'

'E-eh,' Mamavi was at sea. She struggled to understand what her daughter was doing.

'Y-you... y-you must tell me something, Fofo.' Adjovi forced back tears that wanted to drop. Was her mother not coming to take her uniform for her?

Mamavi threw her hands helplessly in the air. 'Ah! Didn't I roam and looked for an iron to... and hang it in the... I'm even preparing banku and soup which you'll take some along tomorrow.'

'No, Fofo.' Adjovi cut in. Apart from seeing her uniform, she was not ready to listen to anything. 'I gave you money. I first gave you one five-cedi note, two one cedi notes, and coins that also amounted to one cedi.' She counted her fingers. 'Six ten pesewa coins, two five pesewa coins and the rest twenty pesewa coins. Yes, I believe. And I later added another five cedi note when my customers came from Keta, Kpando, Akatsi... to buy some of my stones.'

Mamavi was surprised at how her daughter accounted for every pesewa that she had given to her. She drew closer to Adjovi, putting her hand on her shoulder. 'I've washed and hanged them in the drying line. Don't worry. We have a funeral at Anloga. I'll even bring you jollof rice from the place.'

Clearly majority of the supporters who had been selected to go with the debaters were the members of the drama group who would represent the school next term. The students were being taken there so that they become acclimatized to the noisy, tension-packed atmosphere that characterized competitions witnessed by a large audience.

Where was Adjovi? Her eyes red, Adjovi was still roaming every nook and cranny of the village. She ran to Dzifa's hut. Dzifa had by then finished dressing up. She was now spleening herself in front of her dressing mirror. Adjovi opened the door without knocking. Quickly, Dzifa knew there was something wrong somewhere. Upon further questioning she found out that Adjovi had not even had a bath. 'What...What's happening, oh my God? So you've not even had a bath, too? What's happening to you? You know all your people are ready waiting for the vehicle.'

Mr. Otoo-Mensah looked at his wrist watch. They were getting late. The driver started the engine, went on a reverse, and paused briefly. It then took off, blowing its horn persistently to say goodbye to the rest of the teachers and students as well as the parents who waved back at the vehicle.

Adjovi raised her head up. The inscription on the back of the vehicle was *Mega na mo o* which means 'Never give up'. She then stopped pursuing the vehicle and ran back home.

When Adjovi got home she greeted nobody. She bypassed everybody. She gave no respect to anybody among the elders who had come to their hut. As she walked behind their hut, looking for a cup to fetch water, two women cried. Those women were returning from the room where Efo Gogovi slept.

But the women stopped crying suddenly when they saw Adjovi. Aglago, Adjovi's uncle, and two of Adjovi's father's nephews entered the room and covered Efo Gogovi's body in a long piece of cloth. They then waited impatiently for Adjovi to leave the place so that they could carry the body to the outskirts of the village where they would look for a bus to send Efo's body to a morgue at Keta Hospital.

Two children rushed in to call Mamavi. Mamavi and Adjovi followed them. A mad man was wearing Adjovi's school uniform. He was dancing *azonto* with Adjovi's new well-ironed school uniform; and was therefore receiving cheers and applause from a crowd of children.

Adjovi rushed back home disappointed. She came to pick her old uniform that she had thrown away a day before. She put it on and chased the bus with the view to reaching it since there were a lot of pot holes on the road to Keta.

CHAPTER 18

What an evening! A Saturday evening! The students and their few teachers alighted from the wooden truck. They had tied their heads, necks and arms with white strips of cloth. Adjovi was carried shoulder high. Her hair and face were full of powder.

Dzifa and Mr. Otoo-Mensah were the happiest people on earth at that time. Playfully, they threw Adjovi about like a chief in a palanquin. Had it not been her, Konkodeka Expiremental J.H.S could not have won the competition with just three points when they tied neck and neck with three famous preparatory schools from three towns in the district. Luckily, the school spoke against the motion. As she had performed in the Inter-Class competition, Adjovi—although was very late and had missed the first contest—she came to rekindle the confidence of her people. Her confidence and basic debating skills she had learnt from books she had borrowed from library helped her school to come home with the coveted trophy and few other prizes.

Adjovi, Godson and Jedidiah, the school prefect, were given beautiful, gold-plated medals that hung from their necks, making them shine in glory. They were also given new school uniforms plus cash prizes of hundred cedis each. Ten computers were given to the school but due to security reasons they would be brought the next week. Again, Adjovi was given a special award for emerging as the third best individual debater out of the eighty one debaters from twenty seven schools. This helped her to get an additional amount of fifty cedis, a pair of shoes, dictionary, and a mathematical set. Her perseverance and determination had paid and Aganu would be happy for that. Very soon her name would be all over in Konkodeka and even beyond. The celebration continued throughout the night with the children and oldies of Konkodeka singing:

Nenye dekakpui alime nase wo
Nenye dekakpui alime nase wo
Nenye dekakpui alime nase wo

Opɛ no yɛnko nkoaa
Opɛ no yɛnko nkoaa
Opɛ no yɛnko nkoaa...

For three continuous days the people jubilated. They sang and danced *azonto*—a new wave of dance that had dominated every part of the country. However, it was now that Adjovi had realized from rumours that her father had kicked the bucket and his corpse had since been deposited at a mortuary in Keta. She wept bitterly from that day on. She continued shedding hopeless tears after the next twenty-one days, after he had been buried. Although she now had new shoes and uniform she was reluctant to go to school.

'Why should you always smoke tobacco, oh Papa? Mr. Dzinyela and your other friends advised you. But you wouldn't listen. Papa, why should you always drink? Why should you leave us behind?' As she wept morning and evening her thought would come to her two sisters who were both serving in different shrines. The thought of this made her heart heavy, making her lose hope in life.

But Dzifa would not allow this talented young girl to go waste. Adjovi had made her proud. Aside, she had helped her win television set as the person who had trained the contestants. Dzifa would, therefore, go and talk it over with her people so that they would allow the young girl to come and stay with her. Should she come, Sammy, her son, would take her as his sister. Moreover, she would teach her one or two tricks in acting so that she would be able to perform the role of *Juliet* to perfection. This would be one on one after returning from early morning and after school rehearsals.

Dzifa did all she could to get Adjovi to stay with her. She saw her close relatives and explained to them why Adjovi should continue her education. She was a potential student who would one day bring honour and glory to her family. Dzifa was true to her word. The rehearsals were intensified and Adjovi acted with confidence.

One morning the son of Mawusie, Adjovi's elder sister collapsed together with three of his playmates when they were practicing *Captain Planet*. Three days later Mawusie's son was still in a coma. The elders of the family conferred to consult a spiritualist. This was when news spread through the village that the three other children who had collapsed had all recovered. It became clear that Efo Gogovi's grandson was the only person who was still unconscious. He was unable to open his mouth much less to talk.

When the spiritualist came, he performed a lot of rituals. He signaled to Aglago, Adjovi's uncle to step forward. He told him to bring a calabash. He then poured some blackish substance from a bottle he had picked from his bag and poured some into Aglago's palm. The whole place was filled with a strong stench. He breathed out loudly and called Aglago and two others to meet him inside the room where the corpse of Adjovi's father had been put.

'You people must do something special immediately else something terrible would happen again in this household.' The spiritualist told them. 'Great one, what's happening? Tell us something.' The people pleaded with him to reveal the secret to them.

The *bōkō* turned again, still possessed of the spirits. He then coughed twenty-one times. His eyes were bloodshot. 'You people must put something in place else something terrible would happen again in this compound.' The people started crying outside because the little boy was dying. The strange man danced from one side of the room to the other. He drank a half bucket of water. He then became very sober.

He said that some time ago Adjovi's father stole somebody's bush meat from a trap set in a nearby forest. The owner of the trap caused an announcement to be made in the entire community and even beyond. But nobody owned up. Later, the victim reported the case to a shrine at Agbidome. For that matter if nothing was done immediately to appease Gbangbalu, the god of that shrine, everybody in the family would die.

'Look for six goats, five sheep, and ten cocks and twenty-five yards of calico. Add one thousand Ghana cedis to it and bring them to me tomorrow so that I would perform certain sacrifices for you. But remember this: When entering my *operation room* walk backwards. Else you will all join the grave multitude.' Cocks crowed one after the other. 'Nobody should tell all and sundry gathered here that a virgin girl from this household must prepare to go and serve in the shrine.' The items demanded by the *bōkō* were too much. The family elders, therefore, paid little attention to what he had said. How could they surrender another girl to the shrine?

CHAPTER 19

Sixty days came like a flash. Mawusie boarded a bus to Keta. The driver of the bus stopped three times on the way. First, he went to a *blue kiosk* and took two tots of akpeteshie. He stopped again when two passengers set about quarreling

Confusion broke out when the bus stopped for the third time to pick a slim young woman in a miniskirt. The woman was cat-walking by the road side, busily and stylishly chewing a gum. Although the passengers quarreled with the driver for overloading, the driver was adamant and picked her. The driver's mate collected the lorry fares from the passengers. Meanwhile, the driver instructed him not to take any fare from the slim lady. In addition, he asked the mate to buy for her two pieces of khebab from the seller at the market junction. Some of the passengers murmured that the driver had wasted their time. But the slim lady cut in. 'I've not seen passengers behave like this before. Come to Accra or Lagos and see. Come to Afghanistan, Azerbajan, Pakistan, Uzbekistan… and see things for yourselves.'

Minutes later, they reached a place where a cow and two calves had been drawn and painted on a metal sheet and placed along the road. The driver stopped briefly. He and his mate explained the meaning of the road sign to the passengers. They said that there was a *chop bar* in that area where they used beef or the meat from cow to prepare the soup; and for that matter anybody who had not eaten in the morning could get down and go there to eat.

A few meters away, cows and bulls were crossing the road. But the driver had not realised this. While the rest of the women closed their eyes in fear, the driver was still talking with the two women on the front seat.

But they were quite lucky, perhaps owing to the prayers of three mothers breastfeeding their babies. The bus swerved dangerously, skidding off the road before landing in a gutter. It took them an hour before the passengers got down and pushed the bus back onto the road again. They had reached the middle of their journey otherwise many of the passengers would have alighted. Mawusie, Adjovi's sister felt. She shifted from one side to another, praying in her heart that nothing untoward should happen to them.

Soon the driver forgot about what had happened. He kept ignoring road signs, making dangerous overtaking and negotiating dangerous curves. Eventually, a metal broke under the bus. But due to the noise in the bus the driver did not hear the sound of the metal. The mate was also arguing with a pregnant woman who had to add ten pesewas to the fare. He heard the noise but failed to tell the driver.

The driver suddenly applied the brakes and the bus screeched to a stop. Thick smoke came from the bonnet. Some of the passengers began to scream. There were policemen on duty who were checking drivers who were speeding or those who had taken alcoholic drinks over the limit allowed lorry drivers.

The driver gave out a wallet to one police officer. It contained a paper, a card and a two cedis note. Quickly, the policeman took the money and returned the wallet. Immediately, three men and a nursing mother told the driver that they would alight at that same spot. They feared for their lives. On second thoughts one of the students stopped singing and got down. His friends called him *fearoo*, a coward.

Meanwhile, the driver smiled, making 'the sign of the cross' before insulting the policemen. The driver laughed because he had no driver's licence. The paper in the wallet was actually a T.V licence while the card was a 'funeral invitation' card. When he was a driver's mate he observed that good and effective policemen did not talk much. But those who strongly shouted 'park well...park well' actually checked nothing but they were looking for money.

After the barrier he was free to drive any way he wanted. He could press the accelerator to the limit he wanted to the admiration of her two ladies. He took to the middle of the road, unnecessarily overtook vehicles, stopped at where there was 'no parking', and blew the horn persistently for no reason. The driver had started seeing things as if they were in pairs. One front tyre of the bus got burst with two of its back tyres almost getting off their hubs. The passengers held their seats tightly, shouting and screaming. The bus bounced off its lane. An articulated truck fully loaded with timber that had veered off its lane appeared. The confused driver applied the brakes and hell broke loose.

Mawusie's bus somersaulted several times after it had run into the truck. With the exception of one baby and two other passengers whose legs would have to be amputated to save their lives, almost every other passenger on board died on the spot. Several others—including the mate—had their bodies cut into pieces. The driver did not die anyway. Rather, he lost all his teeth and his two legs. One of his hands, too, was broken at several points.

Three days later, after Adjovi's sister was buried, Aglago who had succeeded Adjovi's father conferred with the other elders of the family again. Emergency decisions were taken.

They called in the *bōkō* who had told them what to do to save a calamity hitting the family. 'Yes indeed, Adjovi must go to the shrine to atone and serve for the crimes committed by his father... then her family will know peace.'

CHAPTER 20

The school won the inter-district drama competition at Ho. They were now going to represent the Volta Region in the much anticipated National Drama and Culture Competition.

Adjovi was now a household name. Her name was all over the place and her new mother, Dzifa, was happy for the young girl whose talent would have gone waste had she not come to stay with her. Adjovi's fellow students as well as the elders of Konkodeka respected her to the envy of some of her friends. Parents would insult their children who slept from 8 p.m to 6 a.m to learn from her hard work and humility.

A night before the competition, Dzifa observed Adjovi very well. Adjovi came to stand in front of Dzifa's dressing mirror. She rehearsed a few of the last scenes of *Romeo and Juliet*.

> *'O Romeo, Romeo, wherefore art thou Romeo?*
> *Deny thy father and refuse thy name;*
> *Or if thou wilt not, be but sworn my love.*
> *And I'll no longer be a Capulet... '*
> *Tis but thy name that is my enemy:*
> *That art thyself, though not a Montague...*
> *Romeo, doff thy name and for thy name,*
> *Which is not part of thee, Take all myself...*

Dzifa talked about a few things with Adjovi. She served the special meal she had cooked for her young boys and girls. Adjovi, Godson, Hilda, Olivia, Joycelyn, John Sackey, Lois, Innocent. They would perform *Romeo and Juliet* the next day evening at the National Theatre in Accra. The fried rice and chicken would boost their morale to bring out their best performance because they had not tasted some before. A few minutes later, somebody knocked at Dzifa's door. Dzifa looked at her wrist watch. It was getting to 10 p.m.

'Who is it? Fafa, stop that,' Dzifa scolded playfully at the person at the gate. She thought it was Fafanyo who had come to see her some few minutes ago. He had promised to bring to her and Adjovi some fish the next day. But that person knocked again. This time she thought it was one of the few children who had left their food behind to have a bath and were now coming to eat. 'Who is it?' Dzifa shouted again yet there was no response. Now two people kept banging on the door at the same time. She called Sammy to go and see the person at the door. Two strong, well-built men had forced the door open. Quickly, she sprang from her sofa. 'What do you mean by that...?' How could you just enter somebody's room like that?' Dzifa talked angrily and the people responded. As they traded insults and exchanged words Aglago, Adjovi's uncle entered. The *bōkō* followed. Aglago ordered the two men to grab Adjovi who had looked for a place to hide.

The men entered Dzifa's bedroom, kicking and smashing anything that stood their way. In the thick of the night the men picked Adjovi and took her to where the *bōkō* lived. Arrangements had already been made for her journey to the shrine. She would be tied with rope and dragged to the shrine.

The next morning the news about Adjovi spread quickly throughout Konkodeka. People—especially the school children—were seen standing at various corners of the street. They were in twos, threes or fours. They were talking about the incident which most of them did not believe because they had chatted with Adjovi the previous night. Many simply doubted the authenticity of the rumours about Adjovi.

PART 2

CHAPTER 21

By three o'clock in the afternoon Adjovi and her people had reached Agbidome. They were in the bush where that shrine was located. Before they entered into the courtyard of the fenced shrine Adjovi's hair was shaved by Amegah. Amegah, forty-five, was a chief assistant to Dogbe Vuga, the priest of the shrine. A bundle of leaves called *la* was put around her neck. Trinkets were then put around her knees and ankles before she was wrapped in a two yards of calico. Her sandals were removed and thrown away into the yawning bush.

Led by Amegah the visitors entered through the main gate which was made of a heavy metal. Amegah then offered them some seats to sit. Even though he knew of the reason for their journey, he still asked them. He then got up from his seat and entered a small hut on his left and led out Dogbe Vuga, the chief priest of the shrine. The old priest wore bangles on his ankles and knees with chains of very small bells hanging from his raffia skirt. He had also smeared his face with powder and his fat, protruding belly with white clay. Adjovi turned to look at Dogbe Vuga's long hairs. It was dirty, unkempt and tangled.

She stole a quick glance at the strange piece of staff which the priest wielded in his hand. This put some fears into her heart. The priest sat on a small sheep skin spread on the floor close to where the innocent girls were kept. Adjacent to where Dogbe Vuga lived were the huts of the shrine elders and other assistants and workers of the shrine including one or two lesser priests. Later, rituals were performed. Libation was made with the schnapps that Adjovi's people had brought. This was followed by animal sacrifices and incantations.

At one corner, women and girls had formed a circle; and if one's name was mentioned she would come to the centre. The person would then dance vigorously to a song by mouth accompanied by clapping of hands and simple instruments. The inmates performed a special dance in honour of Gbangbalu who revealed himself through a cold whirlwind that started turning around on its axis.

Adjovi looked at how briskly the women and girls were singing and dancing. She wondered if she would one day be able or made to join that strange team of singers and dancers. Time would tell.

Amegah got up and entered Dogbe Vuga's room. He picked and brought out dried, hollow shell of gourd. This was called *witchcraft pot*. Certain personal items belonging to Adjovi including her panties and hairs were placed into the witchcraft pot. This was to bind her spiritually and permanently to the shrine. She was then forced to swear. Adjovi was unwilling to obey this instruction. She said, *'Thou shall not swear.'* But she was forced to swear. She was made to swear that she would not divulge any secret of the shrine to anybody who might come to visit her and even after twenty-four years when her period of servitude would be over.

The elders of the shrine took the ram, the cocks, the money, and the rest of the schnapps that Adjovi's people had brought along with them. Dogbe Vuga jumped to his feet and beckoned to Amegah to bring Adjovi to his side. He looked into Adjovi's eyes so hard that Adjovi became frightened. She shook back, nodding twice. Was she trying to remember something?

Dogbe Vuga put his arm around her neck. Tears welled in her beautiful eyes.

Dogbe Vuga later warned the young girl again that should she reveal any secret of the shrine to any human being on earth she would surely die that very day. The rules were many. Even though Dede, an old woman, would from time to time tell her about some of the hard and fast rules of the shrine Dogbe Vuga told her the most important ones first before it would be too late. He echoed and re-echoed those most serious ones that she should never forget—what she should do well to remember always.

'As you've come here you're for Gbangbalu... and you're my new wife. You're never to make love to any man outside the four walls of this shrine. Every part of you is dedicated to Gbangbalu and I am in charge. I am *"the eye of the gods"*. I am the only person who has the power to use them... I mean any part of your body... at any time.' The words pierced Adjovi so much. Aglago and the rest of Adjovi's people left. Adjovi began to weep.

Adjovi saw some little babies, boys and girls roaming and running after one another in the courtyard of the shrine. They were all malnourished showing signs of kwashiorkor. Adjovi felt uncomfortable. Thoughts of her twenty-four-year stay in the shrine started immediately. Although she cried in her predicament she soon found herself in Dogbe Vuga's room. Idols, strange images and objects, skulls and skins of wild animals showed in the light provided by the *viebu* that stood at the edge of a huge wooden idol placed at one corner of the room.

The priest pushed Adjovi down, removed the calico that covered her chest before tearing the piece of garment that covered her waist. After thirty minutes struggle Adjovi became so weak that she gave up struggling. Like the rivers of Babylon, tears streamed down her cheeks into her mouth. She lay down helplessly on the floor, thinking about how painful she was going to lose her virginity—something she had been bragging about.

Meanwhile, when Adjovi was going through this ordeal, her friends and classmates were at the National Theatre in Accra, performing *Romeo and Juliet*. They were looking forward to receiving awards and scholarships. How could they make any meaningful impact without Adjovi? Who would play the role of Juliet as Adjovi would have done?

Aganu heard about the whole incident in the night when Adjovi's name came up in his conversation with Mr. Dzinyela. There and then he remembered her fears for Adjo and what might happen to the poor girl. He cried his heart out:

> *As I switch on my television and I see*
> *And I see the naked atrocities*
> > *meted out against those failing souls*
> *My heart bleeds, and I cry and pour away my cup of tea*
> *As I tune and turn on my 'akasanoma'*
> > *and I hear their growls*
> *And I hear about our virgin mortals selling their*
> > *virginities like vanity for no fee*
> *My heart cries. I will forever*
> > *cry out my tears into several bowls*
> *Who will cry with the crying*
> > *Souls—souls so restless like the busy bee*

Hairs shaved, bodies buried in white calico
        they trudge to the shrine with burning soles
Hmmm! tro-kosi now a refugee
        in her own Volta shores with no life key
No pen. No book. No companion.
        No right. No future. No goals
Hold not thy peace oh ye strong men
        and women. Come on a helping spree
Don't rest at the west. From the east make strolls
To the shrine. From Sandema
        to Odododiodio, bring back our girls free
Many shall call your kindness weakness.
        But remember. It takes very strong souls
A man or a woman not to be afraid
to appear weak; you will grow big. Try and see

CHAPTER 22

Two of the guards, Akplor and Apesowa, rushed to the main gate of the courtyard of the shrine. Somebody was banging the ancient gate and so they went to open. Two men were standing behind with a goat, two plain white cocks and a carton of imported drinks. Apesowa looked at them carefully and smiled. One of the visitors looked familiar. The two guards ushered them into the big courtyard and handed them over to Amegah.

Amegah led them to Dogbe Vuga who was mixing some herbs just outside the shrine where some sick people were lying on their mats. Goats bleated. Dogbe Vuga stopped what he was doing to attend to his clients who had come from a far place. He spoke through Amegah.

'*Miawoézo,*' Amegah welcomed them.

'*Yooo…*' the visitors responded.

'*Gbedoname*, Etse. *Efoa*?'

'*Me fo.*'

Dogbe Vuga inquired about Etse's health. They exchanged few pleasantries for some time before Etse set about telling their mission. Etse got up and turned to Amegah.

'Let Great Dogbe Vuga, the only living *bōkō*… understand that I am here again. Let "*the eye of the gods*"… Let the only one who sees the invisible light understand that indeed there is no one like him. Let he whose greatness cannot be comprehended by any living soul understand… Tell the Great Gbangbalu—the head of the gods—that his servant, Etse, has returned from a peace-keeping mission. After returning from Afghanistan, Syria, and Gaza Strip, Etse has returned again from his dangerous adventures in the Darfur region of Sudan

where he survived three bullets. And he has come to thank him.'
Cocks started crowing. 'Let *"the eye of the gods"* understand
that "that thing" he wrapped around my waist is still potent.'
Amegah carried the message to Dogbe Vuga.

Etse presented the goat and the carton of drinks and
some amount of money to Dogbe Vuga. He thanked him also
for protecting and keeping him safely from the jaws of death.

Dogbe Vuga sprang from his stool. Amegah beckoned
two drummers from behind. They came to play some tunes with
donno and castanet for some minutes to uplift Dogbe Vuga's
spirit.

After the dance Dogbe Vuga detected that the other man
who had come with Etse did not just follow him to the shrine,
but for a purpose. After a few minutes'talk, Etse told Dogbe
Vuga that the other man was Atsu, his elder twin brother. Atsu
was a bus driver who needed some protection from motor
accidents which had become common with its resultant effects.
That was why his younger brother had brought him there. From
the horse's own mouth Atsu had this to say:

'"*The eye of the gods*",' Atsu bowed before Dogbe
Vuga. 'Your servant Atsu came here for your unfailing
assistance.' He scratched through his hairs. 'Without mincing
words I will want you to give me powers that can make me
disappear when I come face to face with danger. In times of
danger, I would like to vanish from behind the steering wheel of
my bus and leave my passengers behind. I don't want to die
with my passengers when my bus collides with or crush into
any car or a tree. I will be happy to vanish from my bus and
leave the passengers behind. The reason is that I want to live on
this earth for a very long time because food is tasty...' Noise
came from the far right hand corner of the shrine where some of

the girls stood. They were watching one leper and two deaf and dumb persons who were vigorously dancing offbeat to some solemn tunes that emanated from one corner of the shrine. They were standing in front of one insane man called Abodam who was struggling to get out of his shackles. The heavy chains that hang his waist had been tethered against a big stone; and as such were making it difficult for him to break through them.

The girls approached Dede. They stood attentively with their hands behind themselves. They came to listen to a few instructions from the older woman who had just finished settling a dispute between two *tro-kosi* inmates. He talked to them at length especially on the need to abide by the rules and regulations of the shrine. After she had finished she shared their chores to them. Those who would scrub the bathhouse followed those who were going to sweep the compound. The rest went their various places to get on with their work.

'I know one of my colleagues who drive an articulated truck,' Atsu continued. 'He says he has 'something' around his waist and he says it's helping him a lot. When an unfortunate incident happens on the road you will not find him in the truck. Rather, you will find him coming from the nearby bush or a place close by where the unfortunate accident had happened.'

Dogbe Vuga assured him to consider his wishes done. He asked the man to go and come at a later date. He prescribed one or two items that he must bring along. 'Chief among these items is,' he bellowed, 'a half bottle of fresh urine of a female fowl as well as the saliva of a chameleon.' Dogbe Vuga looked sternly into Atsu's eyes. 'You should also not forget to come with, at least, a fresh tail of a dragon.'

Atsu pleaded with Dogbe Vuga. 'I might get the schnapps, calico and the rest of the items alright. But for the urine, the saliva, and the tail… how would I get them? Even if I squeeze water out of stone do you think I would be able to get them?'

'If I have been able to swallow the gong itself, how much strength will I need to swallow its stick?' Dogbe Vuga asked proudly. 'Getting those items is as easy as A, B, C.' He reassured him. 'A person who has ever chewed the back of a crab should not be disputed if he says he could chew a calabash. I can get those items for you. I can produce those items if and only if you will be able to convert the value of those items into physical cash.' He laughed loudly.

CHAPTER 23

One early morning Amegah came to give Adjovi a serious warning. He questioned her several times. He even threatened to beat her. Amegah summoned the over two hundred women and girls to the courtyard of the heavily fenced shrine. He allowed those who had given birth to new babies in the past week to get back to their rooms. The rest were put into groups of tens. Later, Dede would come and join him so that different chores and works were shared among them.

On the farm Adjovi was paired to work with Akweley—a ten year old girl who was brought to the shrine two weeks earlier. Apesowa and Akplor moved closer in their direction. They threatened to beat them for showing lackadaisical attitude towards their various works. But no sooner had the two guards left than Adjovi and Akweley continued their conversation.

'And so what happened that you were brought to the shrine?' Akweley asked.

Adjovi bowed down her head, trying hard not to cry. 'Actually I... I... I am here because... I am here.' she coughed. '...My uncle brought me here.'

'I, too, I was brought here by my mum and dad. They said if I had not come here I would have died. All my brothers would also have given up the ghost. After that my friends would also have been attacked by bouts of chicken pox. But they said after twelve years I would go back home.'

Adjovi kept quiet, nodding. 'So your father didn't do anything? Is your father still alive?'

'Yes,' Akweley replied quickly. 'What about you?'

'Y-yes...m-me, too.' Adjovi smiled briefly and kept quiet.

'But why have you become quiet all of a sudden,' Akweley turned to check whether somebody was behind them or listening to their conversation.

Adjovi was slow to answer. She tried to avoid Akweley's question in order to save herself from the psychological trauma which might, perhaps, worry her throughout the next few days. 'Why will you be staying here for just twelve years?' She began to sob. She would not stop sobbing inconsolably because she was now very angry. As they conversed she recalled her personal experiences. The first was about her never-to-be-forgotten experience on her first night in the shrine. The second was at Konkodeka—how he learned and did all her assignments so that she would one day win a scholarship to study in Wesley Girls or an equally good S.H.S or go to visit the White House.

'Yes,' Akweley looked at Adjovi's sad face. 'She said I will spend twelve years in the shrine. They also said I wouldn't have come here but for my elder sister.'

'What did she do? What did your elder sister do?' Adjovi dropped her machete and moved closer to her friend. 'Where is she?'

'She *is* here.'

'E...eh,' Adjovi's eyes opened in surprise. 'And you've also come to join her?'

'No. she is no more here.'

Adjovi was confused. 'So where is she?'

Akweley shook her head. 'She has not come home yet.'

'That means she had run away. So is it possible to run away from the shrine?'

'She might be in another village. I think so. She ran away. Didn't she?' Akweley breathed out heavily. 'When the "strong men" came to our hut I did hear them say they were coming to

115

take me here. My big sister had run away. For that matter I should come and replace her so that I would continue with the remaining years she did not serve in the shrine. I also wanted to run away but I could not. I was caught.'

'And so were your mum and dad happy bringing you here?'Adjovi asked, crying. She put her thumb on Akweley's forehead and wiped beads of sweat. Akweley's answer was 'yes' and 'no'. How? Although her parents were quite rich they were equally sad. They had no hope for her return because they had already lost their two virgin girls to the shrine. Their situation was peculiar. A person who had been hit by a white bull before takes extra caution when he sees a plain white cloth. However, they were quite happy because the whole of their clan might have been wiped out as claimed by Dogbe Vuga if they had failed to bring another virgin girl—a third one of course—to come and complete the sentence which had been given some years back. Akweley then narrated to Adjovi how her elder sister had died in the shrine.

'My father told me and my brothers that before I was born, our grandfather, died. After his death the *bōkō* said my grandfather, once in his life time, stole somebody's coconut and the owner of that coconut tree had cursed him. As a result if nothing was done to pacify the gods his entire clan would have been wiped out. He therefore ordered that my eldest sister be sent to come here and serve Gbangbalu, the god of this shrine.'

Adjovi cut in. 'So you already know who Gbangbalu is?'
'Yes.'

'And so what happened next?'Adjovi was absorbed in the conversation. It was pretty hot at that time of the day.

'What happened was that my father said his first daughter was brought to this village, over here in Agbidome to serve

Gbangbalu. She was to serve for thirty-seven years. But after only ten years, my father said, my elder sister started growing thinner and thinner. She had frequent headaches. She also had running stomach. And she would be vomiting, too. This continued and she finally died after staying in the shrine for fourteen years. My other elder sister was also brought here to replace her to continue the service that she had not completed. But after eleven years my sister—whom we sometimes came to visit—was fed up. They say she ran away and that is why I'm here in Agbidome shrine to serve for twelve years.' Tears dropped down Akweley's eyes.

Adjovi sighed, tears dropping down her cheeks. She was moved by the sad story of the poor girl. Akweley continued sadly:

'My parents pleaded and paid some money. He also added goats and cocks before they agreed that I should continue with those twelve years.' She wiped her tears. 'They said they would have added ten more years because of the fact that my elder sister ran away.'

The two got up. They left the place for where Etonam, flanked by her children, was still working.

CHAPTER 24

Somebody sneezed. Another whispered sharply for stepping on a sharp thorn. Etonam turned to look at where the noises were coming from.

'Ei… Adjo and her friend…' Smiling, she waved her hoe at Adjovi and Akweley. 'How're you people?'

'We're even coming to you.' They pulled out their machetes from their armpits. They chopped away creepers of thorns in the path that led to where Etonam had now sat contemplating on what they were coming to tell her.

'Now tell me, my children. Is it something serious?'

Adjovi looked around and said, '*Adoglo lia ati.*'

Etonam kept quiet for some time before asking, 'Did you people say the lizard went up the tree?'

'Yes,' Adjovi cried. 'The lizard is searching for food. It is hungry, and so are we, too.'

'And are you people saying you're hungry?'

'Y-yes.'

'But you've all eaten some porridge this morning? Haven't you?'

'Yes… Y-yes it is… but you know…you know we're hungry and we believe you can do something to help us. Don't you have any food left for us? Food!'

'Food?' You mean food? Etonam wondered whether they were joking or serious about their request. Adjovi and Akweley replied softly. 'Yes, we want some more food.' Etonam forced a smile. She looked into the eyes of Akweley whose lips were parched and dry. She then called Elikplim, his eldest child. Etonam felt sad for being unable to give something to the young

118

girls. She waited for Elikplim who had not come. They were very hungry and so they should start going home early because of the distance from the farm to the shrine. Adjovi's tummy ached.

'Eli... Elikplim, where are you, Elikplim...?' Etonam called out again for the fifth time. The young boy appeared from the bush behind them, sweating profusely from head to toe. When asked whether he had some little banku left he said 'no'. When Akweley heard this she became very sad. Etonam, however, left the two girls behind to get back to her work. It was getting to one o'clock. Things had to be done faster to avoid punishment.

'What's happening over here, Fofo? Look at oranges, pears, mangoes, coconut... Can't we pluck some to eat?' Their stomaches rumbled and ached.

Etonam said, 'I beg you people. I've enough problems to think about. Don't come and put me and my children into hot waters.'

'But we're hungry, Fofo,' Adjovi and Akweley cried bitterly. Etonam took a step into the shade of one of the orange trees whose fruits were matured. But Etonam warned them again.

'Adjo and her friend, why do you want to cause problems for yourselves because you're hungry? You people should not forget that suffering and happiness are brothers. If you've not suffered in life before, then you won't be able to discover true happiness. Encourage yourselves.' She turned to Adjovi. 'Nobody will encourage a girl if she doesn't encourage herself. Hard times never last but tough people do. You can succumb to the trials of these hard times. All you need to do is to be tough in mind. When you're tough in mind you'll be tough in the body, too. Never rush in life as well. If you're patient in life you'll one day discover honey in the carcass of the lion.

'Adjo,' Etonam scolded her. 'You've been here for quite a long time and so you should know better now.' Akweley kept quiet for some minutes before leaving Etonam's place.

When Etonam was returning home she came face to face with Akweley who was running towards her. 'Adjo is dying, Fofo,' she screamed, raising her hands helplessly in the air. 'See... See... Adjo is vomiting. Come and see... She is dying, too... ' Etonam dropped her bunch of firewood; but was unable to run as fast as she could to the place as she might have wanted. She called Elikplim who was at the back of the long cue. Elikplim ran quickly to his mother's side.

'What's wrong with you, Adjo?' Etonam looked fixedly into her eyes which had turned white. The more she asked questions the more Adjovi threw up. Later, she held Adjovi's hand. She helped her to get up and inspected her eyes and mouth and palms. She felt her body temperature and nodded at what she had seen and felt. Next, she put the back of her hand on Adjovi's neck region. When she felt Adjovi's chest Etonam realized the young girl's pulse was pounding heavily. Her baby at her back and crying, Etonam raised her eyes into the sky; and shook her head in sorrow. She shouted, 'Oh God help us!' But Adjovi was still throwing up.

'Adjo,' she said softly, almost crying. 'You're pregnant.'

'Pregnant...?'

'Y-yes,' Etonam was emphatic.

'M-me...? P-p-pregnant...? Tell me something better, Fofo.' Beating her belly to prove her innocence, Adjovi jumped from one side to another. She jumped to where Etonam's youngest child was still crying for food, protesting what the woman had said. *Tro-kosi* women and girls passed one by one to the shrine.

'I can't believe what you're saying, Fofo,' Adjovi cried. 'There is no truth in what you're saying.' The sun had started setting. They were still talking and protesting. But still Etonam maintained her stand. 'Adjo, you're pregnant.' Etonam still remembered her first issue some years back when her parents brought her to the shrine.

In the evening, after they had eaten their supper—their second meal of the day which was cooked cassava and ground pepper—Amegah came. He came to call Dede. Amegah and the rest of the guards—including Akplor and Apesowa—walked and glanced through the crowd. They looked for that particular woman whom they claimed had left the shrine and returned some hours afterwards. This happened three days back when she had left without permission and was, however, seen at the outskirts of the Agbidome village talking to a gentleman—a man wearing a pair of shoes.

'The following people should fall out quickly.' There was a complete silence in the gathering. The frightened women and girls looked into one another's face, each praying that her name would not be mentioned.

'Where is Adjovi?' Amegah roared. Everyone kept quiet. 'If she is around she should come out right now. And then Akweley... and then Etonam... and then the two girls who had quarrelled yester-night... and then...' the list went on and on.

Meanwhile, the woman who was seen outside the shrine talking to a man had committed the most serious crime. She had attempted to see a man outside the shrine. She would therefore have to be punished severely to deter others from attempting to do same. Amegah said and Dogbe Vuga who was listening from his small room was very happy. His chief servant was maintaining the law, dignity, and the sanctity of the shrine.

Two hours later, the drummers brought gong, castanet, mallet, sticks, donno and a few other instruments. There was an exciting, driving beat produced by wooden sticks being struck together. The beat was joined by a drum playing at triple the rate of the struck sticks. Obviously a strong, repetitive rhythm filled the place. Adjovi, due to her natural sweet voice, started the singing while the rest clapped.

Adjovi led the girls as well as the active women to dance. The older people kept on chanting and playing the instruments. With countless variations and combinations of movements of their heads, hands and bodies, Adjovi and her friends danced vigorously and beautifully to honour Gbangbalu. Gbangbalu quickly came to fill the place in the form of a whirlwind that started blowing dust, buckets and other objects away.

The crowd was dispersed to allow the women and girls who were very tired from their daily activities to go and sleep. However, as soon as they entered their rooms Amegah called them back again.

Adjovi cried. She wished she was back at Konkodeka. If she was no longer attending school or if for nothing at all she would be happy to be cracking her own stones rather than being in captivity. But was it well with the village he had come from?

It was not well at Konkodeka. A calamity had befallen that village. Eight children had died and ten children had sustained various degrees of injuries. The boys involved in the misfortune were those who had sneaked out of classroom a day before and joined their colleagues who did not attend school at all.

They went on a fishing expedition with older men. When their canoe travelled a distance of about twenty kilometers at sea, the four older men who took the children to the fishing expedition cast their nets to catch a shoal of fish. But as they pulled the nets the nets got entangled with something in the sea. Three school boys were ordered quickly to jump into the high waters to disentangle the nets; but they ran out of luck. They did not return. The more experienced men who had taken this risky move on a few occasions dived into the sea to rescue them but all to no avail.

As they were returning home their canoe crashed into a rock. The crash punched a big hole into the wooden vessel, allowing water to enter. Majority of the crew members were drowned while a few others—who were mostly adult fishermen—managed to swim to safety.

The bodies of the dead children were washed to the banks of the shore the next three days. It was sad day for Konkodeka especially as mass burial was organized for the youngsters who had lost their lives. Later, Togbui Amekudzi and his elders went to offer sacrifices to the gods of the sea. The full account of the tragedy was given by Fafanyo when he was discharged from the hospital.

CHAPTER 25

Adjovi was pregnant again after five years. She always thought of her fellow classmates, Mrs. Essuman or Dzifa and the prospects of visiting U.S.A and attending one of the best girls' schools in Ghana. But she still had more than eighteen years to spend in the shrine. She was always moody; and as a result bad thoughts, at times, entered her mind.

She would sometimes encourage herself with the little scriptures she had learnt from Sister Saviour, her Sunday school teacher, at Quick Prosperity Miracle Church back home at Konkodeka. Pieces of advice she and her friends had received from Pastor Nigel were also on her mind. She also remembered the words of motivation that Aganu used to tell them when the children of her village went to Mr. Bernard Dzinyela's house to watch television. She also remembered those nights, those Wednesday, Friday and Sunday nights when they sat by the fireside to listen to stories from the old man.

One night, when all her colleagues were fast asleep, Adjovi could hardly sleep. She sat at one corner of her room— the room that she shared with eight other inmates and their children. She leaned against the wall, and thought quietly.

'Nineteen more years in the shrine might be something else, something terrible. How can I appear on *Nyabrōō T.V* like Aunte Baaba Sam to read news for everybody to see and hear about me? How can I go to a senior high school... and to the university so that as Madam Dzifa would say, I could become the first girl to become a graduate from Konkodeka? How...? How...?' She wept bitterly within herself. 'If I had taken part in the National Drama and Culture competition at the National

Theatre in Accra I could have done something better with my life.' She shook her head. Tears stood in her eyes. 'Now look at me... lonely and living in this miserable life for a crime I did not commit. My father whom they say stole the game from the hunter's trap is already dead.' Crying and angrily shaking her head she looked at the bamboo ceiling above as if she was counting them.

She shouted absent mindedly, turning herself to hit her palm against the wall. She put her hands on her head, forcing herself to stop crying so that her colleagues or the guards of the shrine might not hear her voice in that ungodly hour. Her baby woke up, crying. But she quickly put her one hand at the baby's chest, and tapped it gently till it stopped crying. Etonam woke up from her sleep.

'What's wrong with you, Adjo?' She was shocked to find Adjovi still awake, crying and talking all alone to herself. 'Are you sick or you're hungry? I've a little leftover cassava in my bag. You can get up and go and take it. Or you're crying because you're pregnant again? You're too young to think too much. It will affect your health. You may even die prematurely from fear, worry and anxiety.' Still, Adjovi kept quiet, sobbing. She went to bed to deceive Etonam who was comforting her.

Adjovi reclined on her mat, still imagining about her friends and teachers back home at Konkodeka. 'By this time Godson, Lois and John Sackey might all be in school. Jedidiah might be in the university as he used to say. Jedi, I miss you. Where are you, Olivia? A.D Olivia? Oh! Mama Oli, I miss you! Where are you, Joycelyn? Oh Miss Tetteh, I wish to see you one day. Where are you, Hilda? I miss you, Miss B. Where are you my dear mother? Fofo Mamavi, I can't stay without hearing your voice.' She shook her head, tears flowing into the corners of her mouth. 'Where are you, Mr. Fiagbe my favourite Maths teacher... come and teach me *Number Bases*. Wher're you, Virgin Bingo?' Somebody sneezed just at the entrance of the door. It was way past midnight. '...and Fafa, too.'

Adjovi kept quiet. Who might that person be? She thought, her heart pounding vigorously. She listened carefully to the person's footsteps when that person slowly opened their door and entered. Adjovi was furious when she realised that it was Amegah—the man who had tried similar thing on her before. She moved herself slightly backwards. She groped in the dark for the *viebu*.

Like a baboon viper, Amegah crept up on his belly. He slowly removed the cloth that covered his waist. But Adjovi, too, had picked the lamp container.

Quietly, she crawled on one side of her belly towards where Amegah's head lay and had started touching one young lady. Meanwhile, the rest of the people were fast asleep. Suddenly, there was a big sound, '*pum!*' Adjovi never missed her target. She threw the lamp with all her might and the lamp hit Amegah on the forehead. The kerosene in the lamp splashed over his face, some entering his long nostrils and eyes that stuck deep in their sockets. The sound continued in succession. '*Pum...pum...pum...*' Amegah would have loved to keep it cool to himself. But the pain was so sharp and unbearable that he moaned and ran away, tripping over some of the girls who were still asleep.

CHAPTER 26

One Tuesday morning the inmates had a field day. It was a holiday since rituals were going to be performed in the shrine. Dede called the girls one by one to come for their porridge.

But Adjovi sat at one corner breastfeeding her second baby on her lap. She was thinking about many other issues of concern. She had forgotten to see that the elderly *tro-kosi* women were sharing their breakfast. Her wish of escaping from the shrine had assumed another dimension. This had made her grow lean. Her fair complexion was now deep black with rashes on her skin and in between her fingers and toes.

'Papa Aganu and Mr. Otoo-Mensah told us that going to school was a privilege. That was most important thing in the life of every child. They said that if we go to school we would become great people in future. Our children would also become great and important, too. Again education would give us the opportunity to rule the whole world since every president had attended school. And for that matter they always told us to take our lessons seriously. They said we should do our assignments, our class exercises and take part in every exam. I had done all these but why…? But why me…? Why am I still in the shrine?' She cried bitterly.

People looked at her. Quickly, she wiped her tears and smiled to herself. Akweley walked to her. She had gone for Adjovi's food and was bringing it to her. Despite the fact that she was unhappy, Adjovi should collect her three ladlefuls of the watery porridge else Akweley would take it and give it to her two months old twins.

127

'This is your food, Adjo,' she stretched her hand to give the cup of the watery porridge to her as she cuddled the elder twin—whose face looked like Dogbe Vuga. Meanwhile, the younger twin—whose nose resembled Amegah—had lay down, sprawling in the dust, crying for her mother's breast milk. Nonetheless, Adjovi still whispered to herself and this time round people looked at her. Sorrowfully, they laughed and shook their heads for her. But her mind was still far away.

'Papa Aganu said education was very important in one's life. He said because of education America is what it is today. Because of education London is beautiful. Because of education Paris is superb. With Tokyo one cannot imagine how it was created. And what's more? Singapore is competing with the powerful countries in the world... all these were possible because of education.'

'Adjo, this is your food! This is your porridge!' Akweley said once again.

Adjovi failed to respond. 'Even though difficult I must continue my education. Education... Education... Education... I must try every means to continue my education. My education is the future of my dear country. My education, my life; my life, my education.' Wonderful! Adjovi was now thinking like Aganu.

As they took in their porridge, Dede went round. She reminded the girls to hurry up and had a bath. She moved from one room to another, telling them to prepare for a ritual and healing ceremony that would take place later in the day. They should put on their calico. For that matter those whose own were dirty should quickly do well; and wash and dry them before the ceremony starts off. Next, she tasked ten girls to start peeling tubers of yam that the guards had brought from the yam barn. Etonam would join a few other women to cook, mash and mix them with palm oil so that they give to Gbangbalu and the rest of the gods.

'Won't you take it?' Akweley shouted at Adjovi.

'Yes, I must seek my *free*...' Just as she was about to add '*dom*' to make *freedom* the cup containing the watery porridge slipped through Akweley's fingers. The hot porridge fell on Adjovi's laps. It was then that Adjovi realized what was happening around her. The rest of the people laughed at her. She was actually day-dreaming. Her colleagues said, laughing. It was impossible to have her freedom until her years of servitude had come to an end or until somebody should come and buy her freedom for her. They pulled her legs.

After leading the ladies to sing, Adjovi danced vigorously. She danced to the fast tunes that gradually consumed the women, men—who were playing the drums and other instruments—and girls into frenzy. Adjovi and her colleagues were wonderful to behold with their well-rehearsed dancing styles. They jumped, moved from left to right, making deft and uniform movements of their heads, bodies, waists and feet. Their singing, dancing and clapping invoked Gbangbalu whose presence was felt through the whirlwind that blew over the roofs of one of the huts of the shrine. Four guards brought a mentally challenged man. People who were suffering from epilepsy were brought later as the people waited for Dogbe Vuga and few other elders of the shrine to perform one or two rituals.

Dogbe Vuga danced a special dance. After his brief dance cocks were killed. Sheep were slaughtered. Possessed by the spirits, Dogbe Vuga jumped from one side to the other. He entered the small room of the gods. He sprinkled the bloods of the animals on the carved wooden staff in which Gbangbalu himself lived. Part of the mashed yam mixed with palm oil was sprinkled around the strange creature. The left-over was put in earthenware and placed before the wooden creature.

He came out of the shrine. There were two trees that stood just a stone's throw from that small building. Dogbe Vuga requested a bottle each of akpeteshie and schnapps from Amegah who stood behind him. As he faced sunward, he lifted the two bottles in the sky. He said some few words. Next, he bowed to sprinkle those hard drinks on the base of the tree and on top of few stones around.

After he had finished, he covered the trunk of the two trees with a plain white cloth. He placed under the trees—and before the stones—bottles of schnapps and akpeteshie. In the midnight, when everybody was asleep, the gods of the land would converge around the tree. They would come and eat the mashed yam and drink the wine on top. Dogbe Vuga left the court yard and entered the room of the gods again. Meanwhile, the women and girls were busily singing, dancing and clapping their hands. The healing ceremony was the next on the agenda.

The next day seven more girls were brought to the shrine. They were all below seventeen years and had been brought to the shrine to worship Gbangbalu so that the offences committed by their dead relatives would be forgiven. One of the girls was in Form 1 of a senior high school and was going to stay in the shrine forever. According to the priest her late father used juju to kill somebody and took over his farm in his lifetime. For that matter if she did not come to stay in the shrine all the rest of her life her family members would perish.

Another girl, fourteen, was in the shrine because her younger brother who had died a week before was believed to have stolen somebody's farm produce; and if she had not come to the shrine the rest of her brothers would have gone blind the next month. Meanwhile, two school girls who were brought from Keta looked at Adjovi from head to toe. Did they know her? Yes they did.

One Tuesday morning, Dogbe Vuga had some visitors. They were a group that had been in the shrine on six different occasions. They had come again to negotiate and plead with the priest and the shrine owners to release one particular woman who had been in the shrine for eighteen years. She had eleven more years to serve. After three years it was now that they had been able to pay for the woman's freedom to rejoin her family. But as somebody rightly said, 'The tormentor will not allow the tormented to have his or her own freedom on a silver platter. He or she will have to struggle for his or her own freedom.'

Before the woman was taken away, the group paid an amount of three thousand new cedis. There were other expensive items like imported bottles of alcoholic beverages. Final rituals were then performed for her. She was then reminded and warned against revealing any secret from the shrine—especially the deeper ones—to any human being. If she did that she would die instantly. Tears flowed freely down the cheeks of the poor women and girls as they waved at her, wishing luck upon her and her eight children whose father was Dogbe Vuga. As she left the women and girls lamented sorrowfully: *Hede nyuie... Mia dogo... Hede nyuie... Mia dogo...* (Safe journey... we'll meet...)

One of the men who had come and were leaving the shrine was wearing a pair of trousers. The pair of ash trousers was very tight at the man's thighs, between his knees and hips. It was baggy and flowing loosely at his lower legs, below his knees

131

and just above his ankles. Adjovi looked at the man's trousers carefully; and the name that came to her mind was *Hold-My-Thighs-And-Leave-My-Legs*. She remembered Awoézo, her former Science teacher and that particular pair of trousers he used to wear that earned him his nickname. Suddenly, Adjovi stopped crying and started laughing loudly to herself. '*Hold-My-Thighs...*' she whispered as she remembered her days in Konkodeka Expiremental J.H.S.

CHAPTER 27

Adjovi became heavily pregnant. This made her uncomfortable whenever she bent to do common house chores. Since she was in the room that someone hit Amegah, all of them were punished. But she was less disturbed in that she was working in the company of Etonam who had taken her as her daughter and Akweley, her good friend. Those two new girls who, on one or two occasions, told Adjovi that they seemed to have seen her sometime, somewhere were also there.

'And so where do you people say you saw me?' Adjovi put down her axe.

'Eh...e,' the girls struggled to remember.

'Then it might be a different person,' Adjovi said. 'You know sometimes human beings look alike.' She laughed coyly.

'It *might* be true,' one of the girls nodded, shrugging her shoulders. She bowed down to continue with her work. The sky was gradually changing from white to blue. Birds whistled as they ran across to their nests in pairs to avoid being beating by the rain.

'So where exactly? Where exactly did you people say you saw me? And what were you also doing there?' She picked a cup to pour water from a gallon that stood under a palm tree just behind them. Her first child was crying.

'I saw you at Keta.' The girl tried hard to remember something.

'E-h...? Where? Where exactly at Keta?' Adjovi was taken aback.

'A-around... A-around... Around e-eh... no... Yes,' she now remembered something. 'I quite remember seeing you at Keta Town Hall.'

'Town Hall? You mean... you mean Keta Town Hall?' Out of shock the cup of water in her hand slipped through her fingers.

'Yes,' the girl was emphatic, looking straight into Adjovi's eyes.

'Could you describe that girl a bit?'

'Er-erm... she was fair in complexion with long flowing hairs.'

Adjovi forced to smile. 'Then it's not me. I don't know Keta even though I have heard the name before. Her baby was still crying. She turned, wept briefly and dried his tears. She, later, left the place. She then went to take a hoe and pretended to weed; but she was actually crying within herself.

At midday, it threatened to rain cats and dogs. Adjovi and the rest of her people had to rush home. But they should finish their work too.

'So what did you go to do at that Town Hall,' Adjovi came back again to ask. 'I quite remember our teacher once told us that people go there to watch concert, video, drama or attend other programmes. That place must be interesting indeed'

The girl who had now been joined by her other friend, her townsfolk tapped softly at the cheek of Adjovi's son. 'I went there with my elder brother.'

'What did your elder brother go there to do?'

'My elder brother is a teacher. He teaches English. And so when his students went there to have a competition, their Inter-School de... b-bate...'

'A de... de...de-bates...?' Stammering, Adjovi cut in quickly. 'Yes,' the other girl added. 'And I was even there to cheer our school to victory. And we nearly won the competition.' As if seeing that star that occasionally falls from the sky, Adjovi tried to force some false smile in order to hide her confusion.

'And what happened that your school was unable to win?' The girl tried to remember one of the most painful things that their school would never forget in the annals of its history. 'We could have won the competition had it not been that girl we're talking about.' In the course of looking for a cause to cross her mind to remember what exactly happened, she chose a new topic. She then coughed like that bird that calls in the night. 'Had it not been that girl from Konkodeka Expiremental J.H.S we would have won the competition. Before coming here our teacher was trying to say that that girl—who is called *Vijo...Avijo...* or whatever—is even in America.'

Adjovi's body shook instantly. 'Then that *Vijo* girl might be lucky.'

'No,' the girl said. 'She was not only lucky. That girl was simply magician. Even though she came late, she was able to face those of us the audience in that big crowd in that big hall with confidence. She was simply wonderful.' The wind blew the top of one tree against the other as birds chirped sweet songs from the comforts of their nests.

Adjovi kept quiet, little drops of tears coming from the corners of her eyes. She remembered the event vividly.

'If we had got that girl's intelligence we wouldn't have been here by now,' the two girls said. 'We would have also been to America. Or by now we might be in one of the big girls' school in Ghana.'

Adjovi stood up. 'Why are you saying that?'

'We're saying this because we've heard one boy from her school called Godson Dzinyela is now in America. Our teacher told us that after winning the debate competition they later qualified for the National Drama And Culture Competition which was hosted at the National Theatre...'

'And... and... and what happened?' Adjovi asked, almost collapsing.

'They could not win the competition for the reason that the person who was to play the role of *Juliet* was attacked by cholera a night before the competition. She was unable to take part. Sammy, the son of one of their teachers who trained them was therefore dressed like a lady and played the role of Juliet. Although that boy did his best the absence of their heroine caused the fortunes of the entire basic school. But that boy called Godson was selected along with his sister, Lois Dzinyela and two other students.' Would it be Oli and Joycelyn?

'And so how did your teacher get to know all these?' Adjovi cried, trying to dry her tears with the back of her hand. The girls were confused, wondering what might have made their friend cry. Why should she cry over good news for people she did not know? Or did she wish she was like that girl called Lois?

'My teacher told us that she knew that female teacher way back in the training college before she was posted to Konkodeka.'

'And did she tell you the name of that female teacher?'

'Yes. Madam Dzifa. Our headmaster said he would do everything possible to bring her to our school so that we could also act and sing like the students of Konkodeka or that talented

Vijo or *Avidjo* girl.' They stopped their conversation when Akweley and Etonam came round to pack their things.

They had almost finished with their work and the rain had also started drizzling. But Adjovi would think and ponder over what the two girls had said for several weeks to come. She would then try her best to hide her true identity. And would they even recognize her now that her long, flowing hairs were no more? Now that her fair coloured complexion had turned dark and her skin attacked by bouts of rashes and other skin diseases?

Throughout the next three weeks Adjovi's decision of running away from the shrine kept soaring high especially as she had now got wind of what had happened back home, and at her school.

Later, her mind settled on one thing which had occurred to her on different occasions but was afraid to act on. She had to be so close to Amegah and promise to give herself to him.

As she fanned the fire to heat the palm-nut soup which was prepared four days back, the two girls—her new friends who knew her at Keta—brought her baby back to her. Instead of smiling she now cried when she remembered her village and her school.

CHAPTER 28

Adjovi had given birth to another baby boy. Perhaps her prayer was answered. Wasn't it? Although bitter and regretful for getting pregnant she wished not to give birth to a girl who might one day go through what she herself was going through. Meanwhile, her relationship with Amegah—her bitterest enemy apart from Dogbe Vuga—had now grown to be very serious. It was now intimate, hot and more romantic than what the rest of the women talked about prior to the delivery of her second child. She had intentionally saved the small percentage of the money that Dogbe Vuga allowed her to take from the wages of work she did for somebody outside the shrine.

She used the money to buy cream to treat her skin rashes at the expense of her two children whose father, Dogbe Vuga, saw no reason to show any responsibility for their upkeep. This she did so that her now improved skin and face would attract Amegah to love her more than any other person in the shrine. Even though Adjovi had tried every means and promised to love Amegah and the two were already seeing each other she was very careful not to get pregnant for the third time. No. Never. Not at all. Anytime Amegah attempted to do anything funny to her she would cry and beg him to wait for the next six months. At that time her new baby would be old enough.

Etonam and other friends who had gotten to know about this warned Adjovi to desist from such relationship because should Dogbe Vuga get to know about their unholy affairs she would be in hot waters. But Adjovi would not listen to them though sjhe knew that every action of hers was very risky.

Etonam supported Dede so that they gathered together the girls who assembled at the courtyard of the shrine. Akplor and Apesowa brought the sick people who were too weak to walk by themselves. Soon, the drummers went into action. For one more time there was an exciting, driving beat produced by wooden sticks being struck together. The beat was joined by a drum playing at triple the rate of the struck sticks. Obviously a strong, repetitive rhythm filled the place. Adjovi as usual started the singing while the rest clapped.

Later, Dogbe Vuga stormed out of the shrine.There were red and black colour markings on his face which enhanced his facial expressions.The music was intentionally repetitive so that the peoples' voices and movements joined together in an intense, trancelike union. As the people drummed and danced to summon the spirits and the gods, Dogbe Vuga went into full flight. He raised himself to a standing position. He slapped his chest several times as he tipped his head to one side. He picked some herbs from the ground; and started tearing them up and tossing them about.

As he danced like a gorilla, the jingling sound of rattles on his legs, and the ringing of small bells and ornaments in his raffia skirt aesthetically enriched the rhythms of the atmosphere. Like powerful lens, the rhythms focused and united the emotional and spiritual energies of the assembled people. The place became charged.

Dogbe Vuga was possessed by Gbangbalu who had been 'heated up' by the sound of drumming, singing, and clapping. Amegah brought a dark pot to him. The pot contained special leaves, roots and backs of trees which had been pounded and ground together to prepare a concoction.

Dogbe Vuga called for Abodam. He poured some of the mixture in the pot into a white piece of cloth. He then squeezed the liquid into the mad man's nostrils. Five more people were brought. He forced some concoctions down their throats. Blood of animals were smeared on their foreheads and toes. Led by Adjovi the people started dancing around them.

Later in the day, the shrine received some visitors who came to take away their brother whose mental sickness had almost normalized. As they were leaving, some other mentally challenged patients cried. They also wanted to join their colleague. Dogbe Vuga shouted as he rushed on them with a cudgel. They kept quiet at once.

'Now, you,' Dogbe Vuga asked, pointing to one mad man. 'What will you do when you are given a pawpaw fruit?'

'I will first wash it,' the mad man answered. 'And then I will put it in a plate and then I will slice it with a knife and eat.'

Dogbe Vuga was surprised. The man was okay. He ordered the guards to release him from the heavy chains and asked him to go home.

'Next...' He looked at their faces and asked another person. 'You too what will you do when you are given a pineapple?' 'First, I will also wash it,' the mad man answered. 'And then I will put it in a plate and then I will slice them with a knife and chew.'

Dogbe Vuga said, 'Very well. You have also qualified. Go home and join your family.' He ordered Amegah and his colleagues to release that person, too. More people raised their hands, crying. They wanted to join their colleagues home.

'Now you, Abodam?' Dogbe Vuga gave Abodam, a tall mentally challenged man who had been receiving treatment for the past eighteen months—a chance to prove himself.

Abodam smiled as he waited for his question.

'Now, Abodam! You, too, what will you do when you are given a *bicycle*?'

Abodam smiled and answered politely. 'First, I will also wash the bicycle... and then I will put it in a plate... and then I will slice it. After slicing with a knife... I will eat it and drink water on top of it so that my stomach will be fine.'Just when he was about to finish everybody exclaimed, *H-hhhei*... as they looked at one another's faces.

The women and girls went to farm to harvest maize. Before they came there Adjovi had placed a walking stick at one corner in the main yard of the enclosed shrine. On their way to the farm Akweley and Etonam teased her for the reason that she was coming to start walking with a stick. They said very soon she would turn to be *nyangadedi*—an old lady. Around quarter past twelve they showed their palms to one another. Their palms had turned bloody red and were filled with blisters.

Adjovi withdrew herself from her colleagues. She went into the small forest nearby. '*Akpo be yeda de, gake yemekpo ndito hafi yava kpo fie toa.*' (Akpo says, despite cooking palm-nuts, he could not get breakfast which may assure him of dinner.) She shook her head, tears streaming down her cheeks. She checked around to see whether Etonam had come there looking for her. (A night before Etonam had warned her that it was best to keep silent rather than complain and murmur in times of trouble.)

Adjovi cleared around the base of one big tree and hid behind it. She knelt down. She forgot about whatever had happened and then cried bitterly, pouring her heart out onto her God:

Plead my cause, O Lord, with them that strive with me: fight against them that fight against me.

Take hold of shield and buckler, and stand up for mine help. Draw out also the spear, and stop the way against them that persecute me: say unto my soul, I am thy salvation.

Let them be confounded and put to shame that seek after my soul: let them be turned back and brought to confusion that devise my hurt.

Let them be as chaff before the wind: and let the angel of the Lord chase them

Let their way be dark and slippery: and let the angel of the Lord persecute them.

For without cause have they hid for me their net in a pit, which without cause they have digged for my soul.

Let destruction come upon him at unawares; and let his net that he hath hid catch himself: into that very destruction let him fall.

And my soul shall be joyful in the lord: it shall rejoice in his salvation.

All my bones shall say, Lord who is like unto thee, which deliverest the poor from him that is too strong for him, yea, the poor and the needy from him that spoileth him.'

Adjovi wept bitterly like never before. She wept and prayed till her voice became choked. She wept and lamented and cried till her cloth was soaked with sweat and tears.

CHAPTER 29

Adjovi and her colleagues returned from farm, tired. As they trudged to their rooms, Akplor and Amegah surfaced from behind the shrine where one or two visitors had come to see Dogbe Vuga. The two warned the girls from shuffling their feet to disturb the peace of the shrine.

'Yes... Next...' Amegah called the next person to be ready. The last person—a businesswoman—who had entered the shrine had finished her deal with Dogbe Vuga. She was now returning from the small sacred room, carrying a black polythene bag in her hand.

As soon as the woman came out of the shrine, Amegah ushered in the next person, a man, to see Dogbe Vuga.

'*The eye of the gods,*' the man bowed before Dogbe Vuga. 'I work from sunrise to sunset and from Sunday to Saturday. I've done this a couple of years and I have got some money. I have got a woman who is beautiful, humble, respectful and as hardworking as myself. We have dated for two years and I have known everything that a man should know about a woman. I've therefore decided to marry my lover after the *Hogbetsotso* festival which comes off next two months.' There was noise outside. Two girls were quarrelling.

'My Lord—' the man went on his knees—'I have come to you to seek your help. I want to know the future of our marriage.' A cock crowed and flew away as Akplor rushed to the side of the girls to find out the bone of contention between the girls that had made them disturb the supposed peace of the shrine.

Dogbe Vuga sprang up and shook himself. As he shook himself the bangles on his ankles and knees as well as the chains of very small bells hanging from his raffia skirt sounded. He picked some cowries hidden just at the nose of Gbangbalu. He spread the small yellow and white shells on the floor. He picked a metal and a gong. As he beat the small gong, he chanted some incomprehensible terminologies. This put fear into the man.

A few minutes later, Dogbe Vuga started nodding, sneezing, and coughing. He asked Amegah to tell the man something. He should ask him whether he had gone to ask about the current price of a coffin before visiting the shrine. The man was surprised at what Dogbe Vuga had said. He could hardly understand him.

Dogbe Vuga explained to him. 'Despite the fact that you love your would-be wife very much she cannot survive her first child birth. She will die with her baby at child birth.' The man asked whether the priest could do something about the issue, but he said 'no'. He rather told the man that it was the man's own cup of tea. He may choose to drink it hot or cold. The man could choose to obey what the gods were saying or not. The man's fears increased—especially as he looked at the white clay smeared on Dogbe Vuga's face and his fat, protruding belly which had also been smeared with white clay. He left the shrine dejected; and was torn between whether to keep to the *bōkō*'s advice or go ahead and marry her woman. He looked at Dogbe Vuga's long hairs which were unkempt and tangled. What should she do? Should he keep to the *bōkō*'s advice or not?

In the evening of the next day, Adjovi sneaked into Amegah's room. She entered with her new born baby who was ten months old. This she did after making sure that her first child was fast asleep. Taking him along might pose problems for her. Amegah—her dear lover who had waited impatiently for that day—was very happy because the six months period that Adjovi promised to give herself to him was over.

Adjovi massaged, and fondled Amegah's body. Next, she put her fingers into his ears until she realised that the man was helpless. She then wrapped her hands around his shoulders and kissed him. With all his eyes now closed, Amegah moaned with pleasure. By this time Adjovi had her plan work to perfection. She had been able to have her hand on that *big key*—the key to the main gate of the shrine. She carefully continued playing with him till Amegah fell asleep.

Adjovi picked her baby. She stood motionless, shaking and thinking about how to escape from the shrine.There was a sharp knife at one corner of the room. She moved closer and picked the sharp instrument. A thought came to her to stab Amegah to death after which she would enter the room of Dogbe Vuga and attempt to kill him also. However, she remembered what Sister Saviour Savi, her Sunday school teacher once thought them. '*Mega wōame o (Thou shall not kill)... Killers would go to hell.* Another thought came from what Pastor Nigel Sean Ben-Acquaah once said to them:

> '*Forgive and forget... The most painful thing you can do to your enemies is to forgive them for the wrongs they have done you. Forgive five hundred and thirty nine times. Never forget to forgive no matter how painful your pains might be. Failure to forgive will make you a victim of forgiveness. A person who fails to forgive will surely dismantle the bridge over which he must cross over*

himself. There is no weapon more powerful than forgiveness...'

She thought for a while. Still shaking with fear she, unwillingly, dropped the sharp knife she was holding. Quietly, she walked out of Amegah's room and squatted in the thick dark. She groped and picked three empty containers which she had carelessly placed behind Amegah's window a night before. She threw the three containers desperately around. She threw them so hard that the noise attracted the guards at the gate. Two of them rushed to Amegah's room while some went to the side of Dogbe Vuga and the huts where the girls slept.

Next, Adjovi crept carefully through the thick night towards the main gate of the courtyard of the shrine. Adjovi tried with all her strength to open the gate. She opened the ancient gate and got out. But she heard some footsteps from behind her.

To avoid being seen, Adjovi groped for the stick she had placed near the gate. She used the stick to smash the *akadi kpui* that stood at the corner of the gate and then took to her heels.

Just before she stepped out of the gate, she came face to face with Akplor—the man in charge of the guards who worked outside the walls of the shrine. Being afraid that Akplor might kick her to the ground, Adjovi looked back and forth with desperation. '*It is not over until it is over,*' she encouraged herself; and she adjusted her baby which was slipping from her back. Shouting at him, she quoted some scripture verses she had learnt at a Sunday school class:

'*...Thou shall not touch my anointed and do my prophet no harm... He that dwelleth in the secret place of the Most High shall abide under the shadow of the Almighty...*'

She added, '*Jesus is my saviour and he is on my side everywhere I go...*'

Akplor was filled with instant anger. Adjovi attempted to run away. Akplor tried to grab her but he slipped and fell on his back. As Akplor tried to get up, somebody, an unknown person slapped him hard from behind. *Whhuaam... Whhuaam...* That invisible hand slapped him twice in quick succession. Shocked, Akplor turned and bent down to check on that supposed person who might have slapped him. However, another person, another unknown person, kicked his buttocks from behind. *kkiim...kkiim...kkim...* That invisible leg kicked him hard in the buttocks again but now descending in between his thighs. As he moaned and limped in pain Adjovi showed a clean pair of heels.

PART 3

CHAPTER 30

With her baby at her back, Adjovi ran through the bush till daybreak, without knowing exactly where she was going. By 5 p.m. she had ran far. Nevertheless, after ascending and descending chains of hills, Adjovi was extremely tired. Her legs were as heavy as lead. She got to a mango tree. She plucked some. As she ate with one hand she breastfed her baby with the other hand. Tiny droplets of blood oozed from her hands, legs, neck and the skin of her baby. Although painful she rejoiced in her heart of hearts. Her joy came from the fact that she had been able to escape from the shrine. She was also quite happy within herself since she believed she would see herself back in her school uniform in a few days.

While sitting on a hill top, she was able to see from quite a distance. Far away, people, her 'former' inmates, women and girls, passed along. Dressed in calico, they carried bundles of firewood.

'These people are coming from farm and they are going back to the shrine. Fofo Etonam, may the Lord have mercy on you! Akweley and all my friends back there, may the Lord be your guide.' She cried and her cry made her baby also cry. Consoling her baby, she sang:

> *'Tutu gbōvi*
> *Tutu gbōvi*
> *Dada mele afe o*
> *Fofo mele afe o*
> *Ao ne nɛvinye*
> *Ao ne nɛvinye*

Bōŋu bōŋu kpoo
Bōŋu bōŋu kpoo...'

It was a sweet lullaby. Soon her baby was fast asleep. She continued to sing the song. She sung it so slowly that she was unable to hold back her sorrowful tears.

'*My dear child*
My dear child
Dad is not in the house
Mama too is not in the house
Oh my dear child
Oh my dear child
Don't cry
Don't cry...'

Adjovi sang the song over and over again till tears streamed down her cheeks. It was sweet, soul touching and sentimentally romantic.

A few minutes later, an owl hooted. She looked behind only to see Dogbe Vuga on top of another tree, shouting and crying: 'I am Dogbe Vuga... I am Dogbe Vuga "*the eye of the gods*"... Do not run away because you are my wife. Adjovi you are my wife... You silly daughter of Gogovi, I want to see you back in the shrine immediately...'

Suddenly, the thought of going back to the shrine; and the punishment which awaited Adjovi made her fall suddenly. Dogbe Vuga got closer to Adjovi. He looked sternly at her. He wanted to set on her by grabbing her by the neck and, if possible, hit her against a rock in the thicket. Fear made

Adjovi's eyes turn red. She crawled carefully forward as she groped behind for her baby that was deep asleep.

With her baby trapped on her chest, Adjovi started running away from Dogbe Vuga's presence. Dogbe Vuga became furious. He tried to kick her, but his foot touched only a tip of her ankle. This added salt to her wounds. She fumbled over stones. She stumbled over stumps of trees. She tumbled over the bushes before falling to the ground. But anytime she fell she got up quickly; and continued with her running.

Adjovi ran far. But there was no energy left in her. As she sat behind one tree, breathlessly gasping for air, her baby started crying. Dogbe Vuga traced the direction of the noise. Soon he came to meet Adjovi whose forehead and cheeks were oozing with blood.

Adjovi jumped up immediately to run, but was unlucky. Dogbe Vuga stretched out his hand which landed on her back. He scratched, and peeled off some piece of Adjovi's skin with his tall, sharp finger nails. Adjovi fell down on her back. As she continued reciting Psalm 91in her head, she carefully scooped some soil with her hands. There was a shuffle of feet in the bushes that kept increasing in sound.

Dogbe Vuga bowed low to grab Adjovi. But Adjovi acted quickly. She threw a lump of soil straight into Dogbe Vuga's eyes so that he was blindfolded. Meanwhile, Adjovi was at full stretch of her strength. She could hardly run and for that matter she opted to limp away. Crickets and other insects started buzzing around.

Eventually, Dogbe Vuga removed the soil trapped in his eyes. He made few strides and Adjovi was in trouble again. He held the cloth that covered Adjovi's breasts. The two begun struggling until Adjovi ran out of strength. Her entire body was soaked with a mixture of sweat and blood that oozed from her back.

'Who are those?' A voice thundered from behind. It was a hunter who had just finished setting his traps and was going back home. 'Who are those…?' The voice sounded louder than before. Both Adjovi and Dogbe Vuga kept quiet. They looked around.

'Who are you, too?' Dogbe Vuga grunted. 'And how dare you ask such a question…?' He frowned and twisted his lips. Adjovi's baby cried.

'Being a *bōkō* does not mean you have the right to talk to me that way.'

Dogbe Vuga looked at the weak old hunter from head to toe before making an attempt to rush on Adjovi who was panting breathlessly in fear.

'*Tō!*' The old man rushed to Adjovi's side as he asked Dogbe Vuga to stop. 'What has the innocent mother done to you? What has she done that you have chased her all the way to this place?'

'Be careful, old man. Remember, you are talking to "*the eye of the gods*",' his voice thickened with rage. 'And there is no need for me to make a fuss about crushing a cockroach.'

'If the shrine is for the *bōkō*, then the forest is also for the *adelá*,' the hunter responded. 'And if a ghost knows how to tell lies, he must do it on his own grave. For the sake of this child'—he stretched out his hand for the baby from Adjovi's grips—'I will not allow you to…'

Dogbe Vuga cut in. 'If a dog attempts to chew a bone that could not be chewed by the lion it develops an ulcer.' He looked above, chanted some few incantations and swept his hands across the sky. As soon as he brought his hands down both Adjovi and the old hunter fell down, with slight foam coming from the sides of their mouths. 'Those who have made up their minds to travel on the path of foolhardiness will surely end up as corpses,' he laughed loudly as he looked at the two down there with contempt.

Few minutes later, the hunter got up. He plucked some leaves into his mouth. As he chewed them he squatted. He cupped his palm and urinated into it. He washed Adjovi and her baby's faces with some of the urinal. He used the rest to wash his own head and face. By this act he weakened the efficacy of Dogbe Vuga's powers. The hunter then had the opportunity to escape with Adjovi and her baby from the presence of Dogbe Vuga who had not anticipated something of that sort.

CHAPTER 31

Adjovi had spent barely a month in the hunter's hut. Morning and evening the hunter boiled water, added some salt to treat the bruises at her back, faces and cheeks. He also mixed some herbs so that she smeared on her bruises, drank some and gave the little left to her baby. But Adjovi could not stay with the hunter forever. When she recovered sufficiently, the hunter thought it wise to accompany her back to Konkodeda.

When they eventually reached Konkodeka, it was time of tears and sorrows, joy and happiness even though rumours of Adjovi's escape from the shrine had filled the village and beyond. Godson and Lois Dzinyela, Hilda, John Sackey and one or two other classmates trooped to Mamavi's hut in their numbers. 'S-so Aa…A-Adjo, y-you are here. We t-th-th… W-e th-ank God s-s-so m-much for bringing you back a-a-again,' Innocent said, crying.

The hunter met Mamavi, Sister Saviour Savi, Pastor Nigel Sean Ben-Acquaah, Mr. Otoo-Mensah, Dzifa and few other people behind closed doors. Well aware of what might happen to Adjovi and her family in future, the old man advised the people on what to do to forestall future misfortunes.

A couple of weeks later, Quick Prosperity Miracle Church, led by Pastor Nigel organized a fund-raising ceremony. They had a substantial amount of money. A few benevolent individuals of the church and the community gave willingly. The teachers of Konkodeka Expiremental J.H.S also met. They all gave out their 'widow's might' which were eventually added to that brought by the church and the generous individuals in the community.

A few days later, Pastor Nigel, Mr. Otoo-Mensah, Dzifa and one or two other elders visited Agbidome shrine. They went to plead on Adjovi's behalf. Dogbe Vuga and the elders of the shrine were unyielding, but the people begged and begged till midday when their plea was accepted. However, Dogbe Vuga told them in their faces that Adjovi's ransom was nothing to write home about. Their assorted drinks and money were not adequate enough to pay for Adjovi's freedom.

Within the next two months, Pastor Nigel, Mr. Otoo-Mensah and Dzifa travelled from one place to another, looking for financial support to go and add to what they had already paid to Dogbe Vuga. Luck finally smiled at them when they contacted *TRO-KOSI MUST GO*. This Non-Governmental Organization was eager, willing and ready to lend a helping hand. They went to pay for the last instalment of Adjovi's ransom.

For the first time Adjovi started feeling some happiness. The only thing that made her sad was when Olivia and Hilda came to disclose to her about the *black week*—some 'dead news' that had happened barely a year before. The news was about Pious or *Light Off* their former teacher. He was no longer in the classroom. He was now languishing in Nsawam Medium Security Prison. He was incarcerated when he impregnated one Class 6 pupil; one Form 2 student; and one final year girl who happened to be the only child of Togbui Amekudzi, the chief of the village. And so within one particular week, Kafui put together three school girls in the family way.

A couple of weeks later, Adjovi's first born was adopted by the benevolent organization while Dzifa promised to take care of her second child so that Adjovi could go back to school.

As the days passed by schools re-opened. Adjovi's friends started leaving for their various schools. Joycelyn who was in the Nurses' Training College left; while Godson who was a medical student left for the University of Ghana. Adjovi was determined to put the past behind her. She desperately wanted to continue where she left off in J.H.S. It was not going to be easy but she motivated herself to prove equal to the task.

Things started changing as Papa Aganu started visiting her personally. 'Nothing is too late to start. And it's never too late to make amends. Allow the past to die with its fears, worries, anxieties and disappointments. Look into the future with a merry heart and the future will one day smile at you,' the old man kept telling her. 'You can change tomorrow if you forget about the past and focus on the opportunities you have today.'

'But Papa, everything is lost,' Adjovi cried. 'I'm a failure. People are laughing at me. Some of my trusted classmates are running away from me.'

'Take heart, my daughter. I understand your pains. But remember. Failure cannot in anyway be final. And success is always at your reach. It is never ending. Pack the power of positive thinking into your life. Never entertain negative thoughts. Negative thinking will destroy your entire life. Move on in life with good and merry heart. Think positive. Think better. Think pure… And what you consider your sorrowful end shall be your new beginning.'

CHAPTER 32

Adjovi started Form 1 again. The first day in school was quite uneasy. But it was still a groundbreaking event. In her new yellow and brown uniform she walked through the streets of Konkodeka to school. People looked at her with disdain. Many were those who agreed that she was getting out of her senses. Why should a *tro-kosi* go to school? Why should a mother of two leave her children behind and go and sit in classroom to mingle with children she could give birth to? Many were those who bothered themselves with these questions as if they were paid to do so. But despite the fact that people mocked and ridiculed her, Adjovi never gave up. She was determined to go places.

Fiagbe Fiawomom, the maths teacher, wrote *Sets of Numbers* on the chalk board. According to his lesson plan, Fiagbe should have taught *Ratio and Proportion*. But for the sake of Adjovi he thought otherwise. Had he taken one tot of *akpeteshie* which might have influenced his decision? No. That decision would also give an opportunity for those who were weak in mathematics to do one or two revisions for the end of second term examination.

Fiagbe Fiawomom called three girls to stand at one side; and five boys to be at another side. He then raised a packet of chalk and showed it to the entire class. Next, he called one boy to get him some stones from outside the classroom. 'These are all examples of different forms of sets that we can have,' the teacher said. 'We can have a set of girls; a set of boys; a set of chalks; a set of stones; a set of books...' Adjovi and the rest of the students nodded. They fully agreed with the teacher when he finally said, '*A set is a collection of a well-defined object.*' Adjovi breathed out heavily. What an interesting beginning!

Mr Otoo-Mensah, the longest serving headmaster of Konkodeka Expiremental J.H.S felt good for Adjovi. He approached her and gave her a pat on the back. Dzifa, Awoézo, Biba praised her for taken a bold decision of coming back to the classroom. 'Education will make nobody a "somebody"… and change an ordinary person into an extraordinary being,' they told her.

Second term examamination drew nearer than was anticipated. After the end of the exams something happened. Out of forty-three students on roll, Adjovi placed thirty second. Things seemed to have got out of hands. But she persisted. At the end of the third term exams she placed twenty fifth. She was therefore promoted to Form 2.

One Saturday morning, Dzifa and Pastor Nigel met Adjovi. They discussed and considered the best way for Adjovi. 'I've been trying my best. But things seemed not to be working for me. Sometimes too if I go to class some of my young classmates want to dissociate themselves from me. I believe their parents have warned them against coming into contact with me just because of my experience in the shrine…' she sighed.

They would report the matter to the headmaster. But then they first inspected Adjovi's exercise books to find out how she was performing. Though not too encouraging they hoped for her nothing but the best. Dzifa as usual used herself as an example. She impressed upon her to persist so that when she grew she would also be able to receive a monthly salary.

In Form 2 Adjovi increased the number of hours she used to read her books. She paid special attention to English, Maths and Science. In the course of the academic year when Godson, Lois, John Sackey and few other former classmates returned from their universities, polytechnics and training colleges for holidays she approached them. They took her through maths and science lessons. (Those were friends who still loved her even though she had been a *tro-kosi*.) A.D Olivia and Hilda in particular solved some past questions with her, too. They also gave her some text and story books to read at her leisure hours. One thing that she began to love most was when her friends talked about life in the boarding house. She would also love the enormous joy and somewhat independence in the tertiary institutions. She was also happy to learn that Lois and Jedidiah were in the same university. In fact, they were still together on campus; and their relationship had earned them the names *Madam Cheese* and *Sir Lovejoy* (*Cheese and Lovejoy* for short). A particular lecturer playfully called them *Joy Daddy and Joy Mummy*.

Adjovi's effort paid dividends.The end of year exams brought a great relief to her. She placed eleventh and for that matter was promoted to Form 3. She quickly ran to the mission house with her report card in her hand. Pastor Nigel and her wife were happy for her. Papa Aganu, Eyram, Dzifa, Sister Saviour Savi and the rest of the people felt same when Adjovi visited them in their various homes. When others neglected her, these people stood by her side. For this reason she would want to make them proud one day.

Form 3 was a make or break for Adjovi. She took one full week off her busy time table. She used this period to critically think about how she would be able to be on top of the class and also how she would excel in the B.E.C.E which would take place in the next eight months.

'*Unless a seed goes into the earth and dies it cannot bear fruit.*' This was the theme of one of Pastor Nigel's soul-inspiring sermons. Even though it was preached almost a year before how the pastor explained to the entire congregation the second time always made it fresh on Adjovi's mind.

Adjovi's eyes now knew no sleep. She studied her books from sunrise to sunset. From twilight to midnight she read her story books. 'There is more sleep after death.' Dzifa paid some teachers so that they gave Adjovi extra tution after school. On weekends, too, she set out early in the morning to Keta Community library. There she returned the books she had borrowed and asked for new ones. She did her assignments, too. When she returned home later in the day she found something to eat and went out for a choir practice.

One evening when she was going for a prayer meeting, she met Fafanyo who was in a company of some young women.

'Eeei Fafa,' Adjovi said. 'It's been quite some time now since I saw you. Did you travel? I miss you.'

'I am around everywhere. Always I am going to sea and come. Because of that you don't see me in my home.' Two ladies moved closer to him and he winked at them.

'So when are you going to church with me.'

Fafanyo kept quiet and shook his head.

'So Fafa, why won't you start school again?'

'School?' Fafanyo held his waist and started laughing. He laughed loudly till tears dropped from his eyes. 'Ah... School...We are looking for money. You are also talking school.' He continued laughing. 'I am pity you very well. Two children's mother going to school with your children... They say the person who brought school died when he attempted one hot afternoon to find another word for '*is*'.

'If you finish school can you get another word for '*is*'? ' He laughed the more. I am pity you very well. I love you some time ago. But now I am not love you again.' Those two girls joined him to mock Adjovi further. Adjovi felt bad and so she left. She must not stay around to hear one of them call her *tro-kosi* or wait for an insolent, dare-devil teenager to intentionally spit across when she sees her passing by.

CHAPTER 33

And so Adjovi prepared very well prior to her B.E.C.E and for that matter her academic breakthrough was no wonder. In the mock examination she had the highest marks in English, Maths and Science and two other subjects.

When the final results were released by W.A.E.C, Adjovi had the best grade in Konkodeka Expirimental J.H.S. She was also among the best ten students in her entire district.

Adjovi had an admission to one of the best girls' school in the country. Upon series of consultations and few other personal considerations she had decided to offer a course in General Arts.

Dzifa bought a 'trunk' and a 'chop box' and filled them with provisions for her. Few other people came to present some gifts to her. Pastor Nigel then went to pay her admission fee so that she started a senior high school.

On the eve of her departure, Aganu approached her in Dzifa's house. He advised her at length. With a cry of joy he blessed her before finally saying to her that, 'In the midst of multitude never forget that you are alone.'

How Adjovi completed J.H.S was a wonder to many especially those who called her names. Her detractors now respected her in their hearts. They revered her in secret for her commitment, dedication and hard work.

Adjovi took active part in whatever happened in her new school. She read her notes everyday, did her assignments and class exercises. She never played with class tests and end of term examinations. She joined the Scripture Union (S.U) and was also a member of the school's Writers, Drama and Debaters Club. Although she was far older than most of her classmates she freely mixed with them. She never hesitated to go to them. Whether at the dormitory, in the dinning hall or in classroom she sought their assistance when she found something too difficult to understand.

In the final year Adjovi became so popular that the students nominated and voted massively for her to become the senior school prefect. She was liked by her teachers because of her brilliance, dedication and hardwork. Her special talent in acting and performance during stage shows—which was occasionally organized by her school—endeared her to all and sundry.

Four years came in no time; and for one more time Adjovi's hard work paid off. Victory therefore had no option than to smile at her. She excelled so well in the W.A.S.S.C.E that she had a scholarship the following year to study in any university of her choice. How her school would miss her!

Later, Adjovi entered the University. She was now fully convinced that, '*Where determination exists failure can never dismantle the flag of success... We shall all achieve our aims one day if only we attach seriousness to whatever we do today...*'

At the university Adjovi did not rest on her oars. Although there were a few challenges she studied as if her life depended on it. She was careful in choosing friends and associations. She never forgot about her background, too. Anytime she remembered the rough path she had passed before reaching the university, she had a new strength which propelled her to learn even more.

After four years of burning the midnight oil, Adjovi graduated from the university. She worked for two years after which she went back to school to study law.

And so Adjovi became a lawyer by profession. Children and girls in Konkodeka now developed a strong liking for school. Even some adult fishmongers started enrolling in non-formal school.

Togbui Amekudzi and the elders of Konkodeka organized a special durbar in honour of Adjovi. Among other things, she was coming to discuss with the chiefs and elders of the area how they would all join hands to rescue the women and girls who were serving in various shrines in the area.

As she alighted from her Jeep with her husband, a medical doctor, the people of the village welcomed them. They received them with singing, drumming and dancing.

Meanwhile, Adjovi spotted somebody in the crowd. She moved closer to him and the person was Fafanyo who was standing by the support of crutches. His seven children, too, were crying around him for food.

Fafanyo cried bitterly. If he knew he should have, at least, completed Konkodeka Experimental J.H.S. He wept bitterly but was too late. If he had stayed in the classroom he would not have found his one leg in a hunter's trap.

From the durbar ground, Mrs. Mary Dzifa Essuman, Mr. Fred Otoo-Mensah—the longest serving headmaster of Konkodeka Experimental J.H.S—and Pastor Nigel joined Adjovi and her husband so that they drove to where Aganu lived. The new couple brought out a lot of gifts and a substantial amount of money to the old man who was now sick and bedridden.

166

In the evening Adjovi threw a special party for the people of the village. It was all joy. It was unprecedented joy and happiness. It was more than a festive occassion for the elders and children of Konkodeka and beyond. They wined and dined and danced till day-break as they sang together:

Mawu lolo loo
Mida akpe ee
Mida akpe ee
Mida akpe ee na Mawu

Mawu lolo loo
Mida akpe ee...

ADJOVI

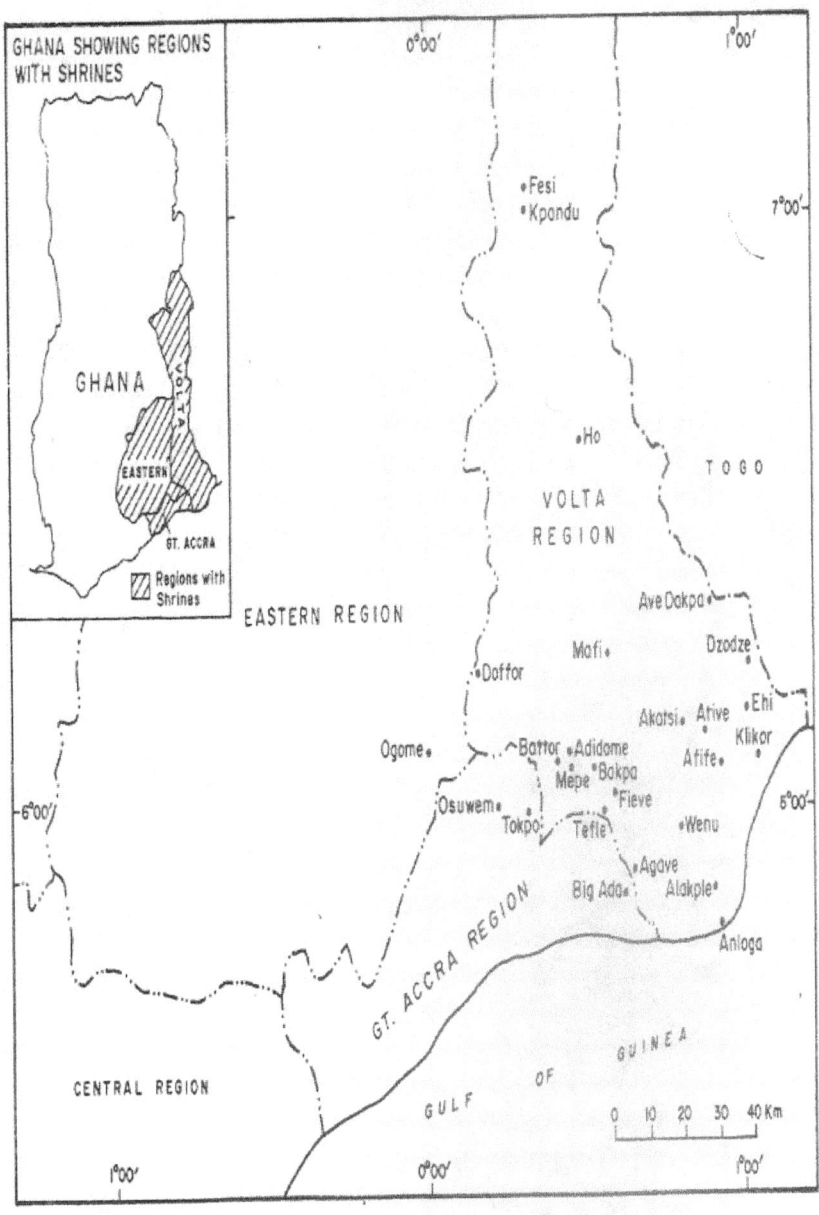

Source: *International Needs, Ghana*

NOTES

NOTES

NOTES

NOTES

NOTES

www.ingramcontent.com/pod-product-compliance
Lightning Source LLC
Chambersburg PA
CBHW061207170626
46809CB00003B/1274